the southern cross

ALSO BY
ALABAMA JANE BROWN

Sinner from the South

the southern cross

A Novel

By

Alabama Jane Brown

Editio Press

Library of Congress Control Number: 2013942665
ISBN: 978-0-9895614-0-2

This book was printed in the United States of America.

www.editiopress.com

For Joanna

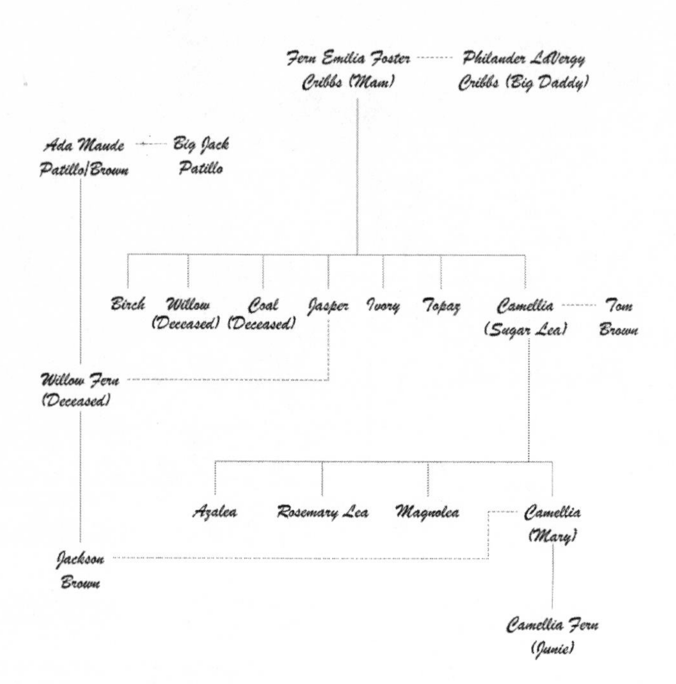
Fern Emilia Foster
Cribbs (Mam)
Philander LaVergy
Cribbs (Big Daddy)
Ada Maude
Patillo/Brown
Big Jack
Patillo
Birch
Willow
(Deceased)
Coal
(Deceased)
Jasper
Ivory
Topaz
Camellia
(Sugar Lea)
Tom
Brown
Willow Fern
(Deceased)
Azalea
Rosemary Lea
Magnolea
Camellia
(Mary)
Jackson
Brown
Camellia Fern
(Junie)

REFERENCED CITIES

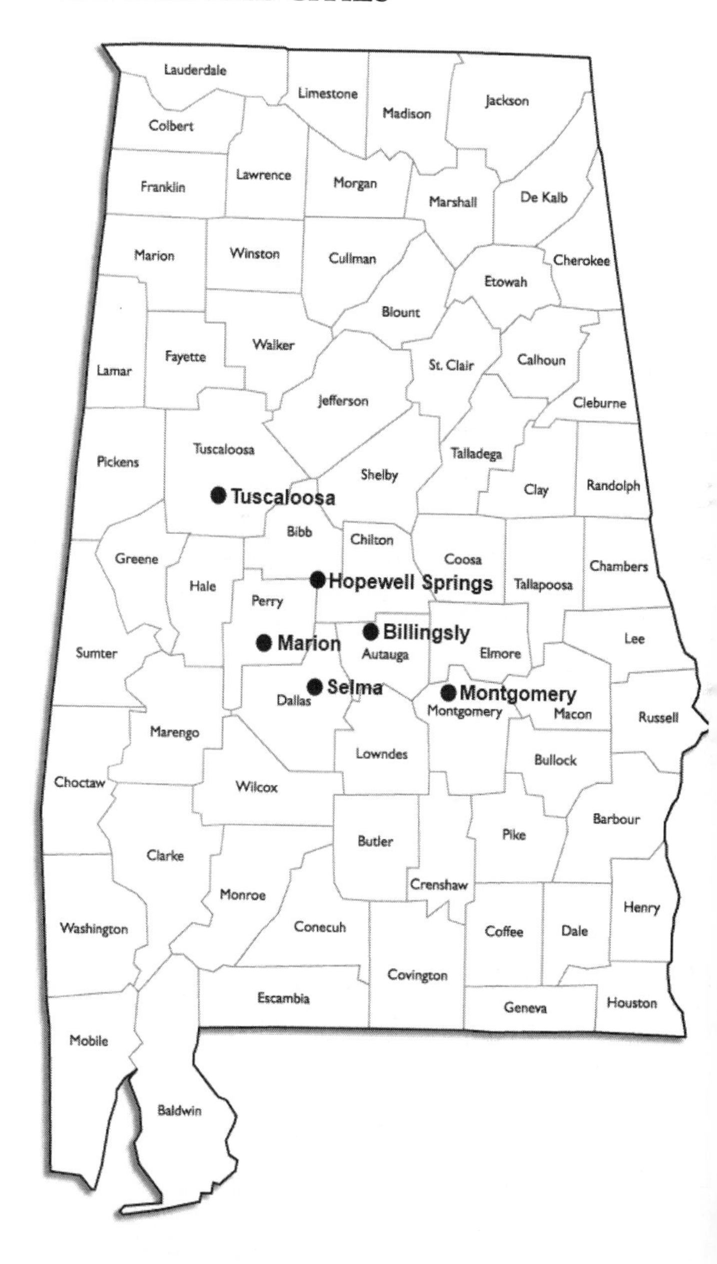

"There are many humorous things in the world; among them the white man's notion that he is less savage than the other savages."

—Samuel Langhorne Clemens (Mark Twain)

"This song is just a reminder to remind your fellow man that this kind of thing still lives today in that ghost-robed Ku Klux Klan. But if all of us folks that thinks alike, if we gave all we could give, we could make this great land of ours a greater place to live."

—Bob Dylan, *The Death of Emmett Till*

January 21, 2003

The White House

JACKSON

"Will that be all Mr. President?" Pauline Johnson asked the President, newly elected just 30 hours and twenty minutes earlier. She stood in the oval office looking back from the portraits of President Lincoln to President Washington and back again to President Brown, not knowing exactly what to expect or what to ask. She had taken on the job out of respect and loyalty, and if it meant doing without sleep for the past 48 hours it was worth every minute just to ask those 6 words, *Will that be all Mr. President?*

"I guess that's all that is required of you Pauline. I can't imagine reading through this stack of paperwork by tomorrow morning, but that isn't your job, it's mine, and I will get it done. I want to thank you from the bottom of my heart for all the work you have put into these past two days. I couldn't have made it without you and your patience, your kindness and your grace. You have been like an appendage I never knew I had. Thank you… really, thank you." President Brown looked down at his watch and sighed a sigh of resignation; not realizing how late it had become and what still lay ahead for the night.

"Just one more question sir," Pauline interrupted his thoughts trying to avoid asking, but knowing it was her duty to cover all things relating to his agenda, "I am still receiving over 30 emails an hour asking about your agenda for the Press Conference tomorrow."

"Pauline, like I told you, it's a secret. Something I should have done many, many years ago; something, now that the election is over, can be covered and not make a difference. Let's just call it releasing a very large skeleton out of the closet, so to speak—but that's for your ears only…

I don't want a word from you to anyone indicating what this Conference is about, and I won't be taking any questions. I have prepared a paper that will be distributed after the conference, so those that listen without hearing won't need to ask again and again. It'll be printed in black and white, and that's it. So, we're done for this day, go home to your husband and have a good night's rest. I'll see you first thing in the morning…" He paused as if he wanted to say more.

"I'll email you the paper just before the conference for you to distribute, so I suppose you'll know first. And I hope you won't think any differently of me than you do now. I treasure your opinion Pauline, you are loyal and that's all that matters to me. So goodnight." He stood and reached out to Pauline and rather than a stiff handshake he put his arm around her shoulder until they reached the door, only when she had opened the door did he release her and send her out into the night, where snow was falling and bright lights lit her path like magic.

Her mother sacrificed everything for Pauline, working as a cleaning woman, raising other people's children, even ironing other people's clothes well into the darkest part of the night so Pauline could have an education. Now Pauline was the Assistant to the President of the United States. The circle was complete.

President Brown sat down at his desk and tried to fuse words together in his head. Should he ask for forgiveness? Should he simply state the facts, be blatant and make his statement with a quiet resolve? He knew he should seek the counsel of his three sons—all great writers and orators in their own right—or perhaps ask his wife Ava, but in the end he knew it rested with him alone.

He pulled out a package of letters tied together in a plain white cord from his desk and studied the first letter from her. Her simple handwriting was endearing, her spelling still crude and untouched by anyone. He knew the letter was her way of keeping the promise, *I will write you every day for the rest of my life Daddy*. She made the promise on their first meeting, and now he would be introducing her to the world, his daughter, his most treasured secret, the crosshatched longing to give her a birth again into a world she deserved.

There would be more than a week of love; they would finally have a lifetime. And so he began. ...Good morning Ladies and Gentlemen I want to introduce to you today a member of my family I have failed to acknowledge in the past, not out of fear of rejection or persecution from you, the great people of the United States, my fear was that I would have to share her with you, and all I ever wanted was to be alone with her, watch her speak her first words, help her ride her first bicycle, and shoulder her from the burden of injustice due to her color. I have failed her, and I have failed all of you...

MAM

My life has been beautiful. Although at times the circumstances surrounding my life have not always been kind to me, I can say, all in all, life *is* worth living.

As I lay dying—perhaps it is my last day—I cannot utter one word to those who surround me and fuss over me on this, the eve of my one-hundredth birthday.

I remember my birth. Most people never believed me when I told them I remember the moment when my head, then one shoulder at a time, my thick well-formed torso and finally my skinny little bird legs slid with ease from my

Mother's safe womb into the world. But I do remember the moment, and I have remembered every moment since with the ease of an elephant.

I remember my birth and I will remember my death. I feel the shadow of death growing closer to me now. Soon the light will drain itself from my room and even the splendor of the evening star will be gone from my sight. I will miss the sunshine. In Heaven I can see the sky is a pale, pale blackness that surrounds you like a warm blanket on a winter night. I always dreaded winter; so I suppose I might be dreading Heaven a bit also. I cannot imagine living forever under the weight of goodness and—perhaps—self-righteousness. I have sinned on many occasions and been too stubborn to ask forgiveness. I held grudges against God when I buried two children. I took God's name in vain. I had too much wine on many nights to keep me company until the sweetness of the vine led me into a deep sleep where I dreamed of my husband dancing under the weight of a perfect moon, only to wake with a headache and the sad memories again flooding me with their cold vengeance. I pray now for forgiveness Dear Lord, hear my feeble prayer and lead me to Heaven, where I pray I will be greeted by my husband, and my two dead children, and all the others who have gone before me. Please let me see them.

My mind is still clicking and turning; I wish I could sleep and rest my mind, for my body has shut down. And the voices around me speak as if I will go on for at least one more day; they speak of the party they have planned.

They say an elephant never forgets. I would like to forget some of my memories. The pain of losing two children, one before I even knew her, the other lost because of the recklessness of youth and the cruelty of fate.

I was born on June 20, 1863. It was a cool evening for Alabama, on the cusp of summer. My Mother was a loving, God fearing woman who loved God's nature above all else. She named me Fern Emilia for I was born on the banks of the Alabama River surrounded by an abundance of ferns, amid the exquisite flora and fauna that inhabited Alabama in the mid 1800's. There were forests of tall, proud Mahoganies and Elm, Chestnut, lean straight Poplars, and the forgiving Pines which dotted the landscape with their promise by remaining evergreen. Ever present.

My Mother told me she calculated my birth in accordance with a particular fern she watched sprout and grow more beautiful each day, and knew when the fronds reached the tips of the low hanging Water Oaks, her time would come and I would be born. When I was five, she and I wandered to the fern; dug it from the rich, black soil, wrapped it up in a potato sack and carried it to our home where we planted it beside our back steps alongside the pebble path which led to the vegetable garden. The fern grew taller and sturdier each summer, until the town was burned, then I suppose it too died like so many of the town's people—including my dear Mother.

Having been born in the middle of the war, which tore apart our country like an angry wound ripping apart a body, I was a survivor from the beginning. My birth left my poor Mother weak and sick. She developed a strong case of the "all over dropsy", as she liked to call it, but I remember nothing but pure love. We lived good compared to most people in our county.

My Daddy made buggies and we always had a fair amount of money and nice things to make our home beautiful and comfortable, but the war changed so much of our life and our way of living. We didn't see much war action, there were always deserters and even some Yankees who came through town. We were like an oasis to ourselves, and I sometimes think maybe God saved our town only to destroy it later with His own way of taking away.

As I said, I grew up living in Erie, Alabama on the banks of the Alabama River. Erie was an important town. It was midway between Mobile Bay and the mouth of the Tennessee River making it an important stop for the river boats that brought prosperity and civilization to the South. We had a wonderful family life. Daddy was one of the more important men in Erie and his craft of buggy making made our home and his workshop a hub of excitement and trade. Erie was prospering well after the war. Everything seemed perfect until a young slave from Mobile entered Erie one fateful day in 1876 carrying with him a lethal case of yellow fever. Within two weeks more than three-fourths of the townspeople were dead, including my mother and my four sisters. My daddy packed me into a buggy, and we made a tearful journey north to our new home, Hopewell Springs. When we left Eerie, riding out of the ghost town, burning bodies piled in mass graves alongside the river, we were saying good-bye to a way of life we would never see again. The slaves were free at last. We had our share of slaves who helped Momma and Daddy in his buggy business. Daddy let the slaves go free and now they are living among the ghosts. I know I will see Momma again, as plain as day; she will come back to me if only in my dreams. This is my only prayer to God, let her come back to me. That is my request. Come back to me. Yet onward we move, north. Daddy says we will know the right place to settle when we get there, and we must rebuild our lives just as our country rebuilds.

I was almost thirteen years old and already I felt I lived a life so full even death could not kill my spirit. I watched the smoke of Erie burning behind me and even today, as I lay dying, I see only the green eternal beauty of Erie. The rich haunting of a ghost town still smoldering on the banks of the river. Hundreds of hastily dug graves, some without markers, some poor bodies buried without even caskets. Death was cruel that summer. I remember the black richness of the soil, a city lying dead center in the Alabama Black Belt, the earth so dark cotton grew as tall as pines, and pines as tall as eternity. I remember the graceful tenderness of my mother, the laughter of my sisters and the hope of the future.

I have always believed hope is the sustenance of life. Hope is desire with expectation, and hope is a tangible emotion, just as filling as bread. For Paul said in his letter to the Corinthians, "and now these three remain: faith, hope and charity. But the greatest of these is charity". I will argue with Paul when I arrive in Heaven that the greatest of these is hope, for without hope there could never be faith or charity. Hope has kept me alive and hope will be my friend tonight when I die.

I fear another war is coming, brought on by the ignorance of fear, our governor George Wallace and his notions about what is right and wrong and acceptable to the people of my state. I fear for my precious surviving children and especially for Junie, my great-granddaughter. My sweet Junie, born on my birthday. God's gift to me and to all of us who know her and love her. I hear her calling my name, but I can't answer. I can't answer. I know she must see the tears that are springing from my cloudy eyes. If only I could tell her to be brave and have hope. If only I could tell her I will see her again. I will see her in the greenness of spring, in the blue skies of summer, in the smallest act of love I will be watching over her. God will at least let me have that. I earned it.

KINGS PARADISE

June 19, 1963, *Juneteenth*

TOM BROWN

Tom Brown sat in the white washed rocking chair lending himself to the will of the universe. He was at peace. At rest. Some people called him a saint; other's called him a fool. He figured he was in the middle, a little of both. It was difficult to maintain a masculine identity in a house with six women, ranging in age from nine to ninety nine. The oldest, his mother-in-law Mam, and the youngest, his granddaughter Junie, were both one day shy of their common birthday. In the middle were his wife's sisters, Ivory and Topaz, and of course his wife, Sugar Lea, officially named Camellia, in keeping with the line of family matriarchs. Ivory and Topaz were the outcast sisters named for nature's bounty, gemstones, purity.

Tom was content and considered himself an anchor holding down the whimsies and far flung dreams of the household of women. He loved them all in separate places in his heart. His love for Sugar held the five-starred place in his heart, and helped him to know and understand the others, giving him reason to love them without judgment and pain. He had known sorrow and strife, and he had known bigotry and hatred most of his life, but he chose love for all mankind. The matriarch of his life was Mam, Sugar's mother, tomorrow looking at her 100th birthday full in the face, and the shadow of death which Tom felt had been circling the house for weeks like a flock of vultures. He admired Mam and felt as if he too had been captive inside her holy womb like one of the sisters. She was the ship to Tom's anchor, the seasoned wood to his fires, the land to his imaginary tumbleweeds.

The rocking chair slapped the floor, off kilter, it needed to be mended, the joints needed a liberal dose of wood glue and clamps, a few screws in the hand rests would help reinforce the chair and give the seated a much better sense of safety. The women avoided it fearing it would collapse at any moment and land them in the hospital with a broken hip, or worse, a broken pelvis. Tom avoided fixing the chair, it was his one private place to retreat when emotions ran on the juice of high octane hormones. He realized, with Junie's birthday tomorrow, he would soon have a teen-ager in the house again; he dreaded the highs and lows of heartbreak for her and the emotional outlet her voice would lend to the already hormonal intonations in the house. At best, his hearing would become worse than now and he would live in a place of silence and contentment, knowing her heartbreak by looking into her lovely yellow eyes. He would be there for her as he had been for her mother, his youngest daughter Camellia, who changed at age 13, almost overnight, into a woman on her own lonely journey to places Tom could not visualize or understand, certain she had become possessed by some alien creature. She even changed her name to Mary because she said she wanted to remain anonymous, and carrying the weight of the name Camellia inferred too much of a family burden to carry. He realized everyone at his home, King's Paradise, slipped into their names each morning as if putting on their dress for the day.

The smallest constellation is The Southern Cross. Crux Australis is the scientific name. The Southern Cross lies inside the Milky Way and is surrounded by the constellation Centaurus on three sides.

—enchantedlearning.com

June 19, 1963

JUNIE

Tomorrow I will be ten. Tomorrow my great-grandmother—Mam—will be one hundred. My grandmother Sugar Lea, Mam's baby daughter, although she is not technically a baby any longer because she is almost sixty seven, but Mam still calls her "Baby-girl"; anyway, Sugar Lea is having a huge birthday party to celebrate our birthdays and Juneteenth, the official day of the end of slavery. I have been blessed that my entire family has always honored the colored people, and Juneteenth is always celebrated as a part of my birthday and Mam's birthday. I know I am getting my first tube of lipstick, and hopefully a canopy bed of my own like the one Mam sleeps in. Mam only gets to be one hundred, because that, in itself, is a gift.

Mam is big on names and nicknames, my nickname is Junie. One day she looked up at me, while I was turning cartwheels in the front yard, and called out to me from her perch, sitting just as pretty as a canary dressed in the yellow shirtdress she probably owned for the past forty years, and it fit her perfectly because she had never gained more than one ounce in all her adult years. She existed on turnip greens and cornbread, and drank warm water, that was all she allowed herself to eat, and of course her mainstay, tomato pie; she invented it, she claimed, and there was always a cupboard full of them in case someone had a baby or someone died. She was always the first one there with a tomato pie and advice on how to raise the baby or how to grieve to get all the pain out. She had answers to all questions, and a gift for making the smallest person feel important. Anyway, she looked at me from her perch on the front porch and hollered out that I looked just like a June bug tumbling around in the grass. From that day on, I became June Bug, Junie Moon or Baby, depending on who was talking to me, except my mother, who calls me by my full Christian name, Camellia Fern.

My daddy is dead. We do not speak of him in my house because… I don't know why. I personally never knew him, and have never seen a photograph of him. All I know is he deserted my mother before I was born. I'm not even sure if he is technically dead, but in my mother's heart he is dead, so I suppose he is dead even though I would like to know for certain. I know better than to bring up his name or his memory because when I do my mother gets a sad look on her face and that tells me to keep my mouth shut. Actually, the entire family avoids speaking of my father. I feel you have a right to know something about your heritage, but in my case, I learned I must put off knowing anything about him. At least for now. I feel he is alive. I find it strange that there are no photographs of him lined across the mantle or on the top of the grand piano that sits in the parlor of our big house. It is as if he never existed. However, I know he did because there *is* after all—me. I think I must look like him because I do not look like my mother or anyone else in my family at King's Paradise.

I am dark skinned, or olive as Sugar Lea likes to call it, with thick black hair, and my eyes tend to be green, or almost yellow, depending on what color I am wearing. My hair is heavy and course and I wear it down my back in one long braid and have worn it this way since I can remember. My grandfather tells me that my hair, my braid, is a medal I should wear proudly. I have wanted to chop my hair off a million times, but none of my family will allow it. Therefore, I am obligated to wear my medal and be proud of it I suppose.

We have many Cherokee and Creek Indian descendants in our family and I suppose my hair represents the departed ones before me. I do not mind my hair so much, but I would like to try and wear it in another style that looks more grown-up.

I wonder if my daddy has the same black hair and yellow eyes, but I never looked into his eyes and saw a reflection of my soul, and I never will. I have missed him and at times felt orphaned; yet because most of my life I was raised by Mam, Sugar Lea and Ada Maude (my black mother), I have not been an orphan.

There is a difference, feeling like an orphan and being one. Orphans are a lost lot in life, drifting and clinging onto anything and everything which comes their way. I could have been a total tomboy by now, were it not for Mam; she insisted I was always a lady first. I could not even say "darn" or "shoot" around her. Mam was in the third graduating class of Judson College for Women. She studied Shakespeare and Thoreau. She wanted Walden Pond, and got it by marrying Big Daddy and coming to live at King's Paradise.

King's Paradise is an old, drafty house which at best resembles an anchored ship. It is safe and beautiful here in every season, with every light that floods it. First morning sun is the most beautiful to me, but even in the moonlight there is a beauty that is hard to define. You just have to be here to understand the beauty. Poems, essays, even photographs do not do justice to the way light transforms this old house. My grandmother keeps the house lit mostly by kerosene lanterns. There is the glow of the blue television light, which streams throughout the big den on the back of the house that was remodeled five years ago. We got electricity here only ten years ago, the year I was born. It wasn't a question of whether or not we could afford it; it was a question of beauty and aesthetics. I suppose the interior of the house is most beautiful at night all lit up with the amber glow of kerosene lanterns and candles. I love it here. This old, crooked house where nature meets modernism. We finally got a real electric stove two years ago, and now our clothes smell free of the ever-clinging wood smoke. I miss the wood stove, but my Mother doesn't, because it was the one chore delegated to her: stacking the hickory, oak and locust in the wood shed. She preferred this chore because it was mindless and kept her in shape. She has an aversion to exercise and prefers to think of herself as some kind of pioneer woman; come to think of it, all the women at

King's Paradise consider themselves a pioneer spirit.

My mother's real job is a professor at the University of Alabama, sixty miles away in Tuskaloosa. She is real smart, and even though she loves me, she is too busy most of the time to deal with me. I understand, but I do wish just once she could look me full in the face, like Sugar Lea and Mam do, and see the real me.

My mom is an astronomer, and Sugar Lea says most of her life she had her head in the stars. I know all the constellations, and can find the North Star in a New York minute, but it is hard to compete with such a stellar sky for my mother's attention. I laugh about it some days, and other days I cry. It is tough to justify knowing your mother prefers the company of the North Star to your own.

Momma needs the stars as much as she needs food, water and shelter. She is a wanderer by nature, a sense of permanence is lacking in her soul. Sugar Lea says Momma lacks roots to ground her, which is the reason her head is always in the sky with the stars. Momma set her eyes on the horizon many years ago, but for Momma, the horizon seems to be ever changing, just like the location of her favorite constellation, the Southern Cross.

It is hard, almost impossible, to find the Southern Cross in the Alabama sky on most nights because it is technically only visible in the Southern Hemisphere, and even though Alabama is southern, it is not in the Southern Hemisphere. However, Momma waits all year for the month of June to arrive so she can hope to glimpse the Southern Cross. On warm June evenings she carries me on her back across the pasture, which smells of rabbit tobacco and cow manure, where we find a perfect patch of crimson clover and sit ourselves down to find the Southern Cross.

Momma thinks the Southern Cross is the new Star of Bethlehem because thousands of years ago the four major stars that make up the Southern Cross were the object of reverence by wise men just like the ones who visited the Baby Jesus. At that time, the Southern Cross was visible at the horizon; then suddenly the constellation just disappeared. Momma thinks the Southern Cross went away when Christ was crucified, and she believes when it is visible to everyone on earth, then and only then, peace will finally come for good. It is believed that European explorers rediscovered the Southern Cross and made it an official constellation. For many years the Southern Cross was actually a part of the constellation Centaur's feet; the Centaurs in mythology were part man and part horse. One Christmas, when I was very young, I told Momma all I wanted was a Centaur. I really believed they existed; now of course I know they really do not exist at all, and I'm probably the only person in my class who knows what a Centaur is. Mam thinks mythology is very important and teaches us great and wonderful life lessons. She questions what myth is, she believes reality is myth in disguise, and she believes God is gravity, which is the missing link in Einstein's theory. Momma does not necessarily buy into theories of astronomy or physics at all. She believes the Southern Cross is there to save us all from hell and damnation. She says when the Southern Cross rises high in the heavens everything will be good again with the world.

> *Many believe the Southern Cross effect will begin to appear in the year 2007 as the constellation begins to brighten again. Some prophets believe the "End Times" events end in 2007, possibly resulting in Armageddon. Hope for the world will come from the Southern Hemisphere. This brightening supernova could be the new Star of Bethlehem.*
>
> —greatdreams.com

Lately, Momma worries about Governor Wallace and his attitude toward the Negroes. Momma has many Negro friends, and some days they all stop by the house and Sugar Lea fixes them a glass of iced tea. She does that for everyone, and I reckon she would do the same for George Wallace if he would ever stop by King's Paradise.

On warm June nights, Momma is at her happiest. It does not take much to make her happy, just stars and justice. She likes the Southern Cross even though it is the smallest constellation in the heavens, and maybe that is why Momma likes it so much, because she is always a fighter for the smallest of things that do not matter, the underdogs. This is why it is hard for me to understand that she never seems to notice me.

I am named after my grandmother, Camellia (Sugar Lea) and my great-grandmother Camellia Lea Cribbs. Camellia Cribbs was the daughter of Daniel Edward Cribbs, the first official sheriff of Tuskaloosa County, Alabama and the first stoneware manufacturer in the entire state of Alabama. (I hope you don't get confused with all the Camellia's. We are better known as one, two and three. It makes life easier, going by the numbers.)

Anyway, I guess Daniel Cribbs figured you had to keep the peace and make the vessel to keep it in. He made wine jugs, which he never really owned himself because he was also a deacon at the First Baptist Church of Tuskaloosa, and anyone in their right mind knows Baptists do not drink anything stronger than iced tea with homegrown mint.

Sugar Lea had three sisters, one deceased, and two brothers, one deceased. Her brothers were born first. They are all named after things of the earth, as Mam likes to say, because she says the earth is holy and all God's creatures must be named something that was around when God created the earth.

She is not big on biblical names. Although, since her Shakespeare period is over, the Bible is now the only book she ever reads. She thinks big chunks of the Bible are missing somewhere because she wonders how we really know anything, or who really cares who begot who, and all that stuff is just filler.

She believes God is neither a man nor a woman, she believes God is just God and real goodness and she argued her whole life that God *is* gravity. She was around when Einstein published his *Theory of Relativity* and Big Daddy—Mam's husband—spent a lot of time reading about it and what it represented. He was very smart for a country man; he preferred living in the country and growing things to living in a city and being crowded out by things. Things really do not matter in the scheme of the universe but sometimes the right things are nice to have, especially if they are beautiful.

I think my mother is an Astronomer because of Mam and Big Daddy. She got her mind from listening to Mam and Big Daddy all those years they were raising her. Mam raised everyone in our family in some way. Nieces, nephews, cousins, even some down-and-out townspeople have at some time found their way to her big loving home.

Mam has only one religion and that is the Golden Rule. She also says it is plainly written in the Good Book that the only true religion is helping widows and orphans, and all that other stuff is just filler. The only piece of art Mam owns is a needlepoint sampler that hangs over her bed; it reads:

"He who has two coats, let him share with him who has none, and he who has food, let him do likewise."

—Luke 3:11, The Holy Bible

She would never, ever, in any way want to offend God and His majesty, but she is pretty angry at the way mankind has ruined God's word by making it work for their own advantage. She said Jesus would never drive around in a Cadillac. We laugh at her wisdom, but anyone who is privileged enough to listen to her will surely see the love of Jesus just oozing out of her eyes.

Tomorrow, Sugar Lea has the entire family coming over to our big, old house to celebrate our birthdays and Juneteenth. Mam's real name is Fern Emilia but Mam suited her, and that is what we always called her. Fern is a pretty name, and Sugar Lea says Mam's own Mother (she was one-half Cherokee) was a lot like Mam regarding names. Names say a lot about a person.

We are a family of strange names, and I guess you could say, strange people. Most of the people in Hopewell Springs—that is where we all live, Hopewell Springs Alabama—think we are a strange group. There are a lot of us. Most of us have a name that ends with "lea", which my grandmother came up with for her children. My Mother's sisters are Azalea, Rosemary Lea, Magnolea and my mother Camellia named after my grandmother. But my Mother changed her name to Mary the year I was born. Do not ask me why.

Mam named all six of her children from various kinds of nature things. First, there is Uncle Birch, because Mam loves Birch trees. She actually talks to them; she thinks they are sacred. Uncle Birch had a twin sister who died at birth, and my grandmother named her Willow. Willow is buried behind Mam's root house, a place she kept her root vegetables such as beets and potatoes; she also kept her scuppernong wine there. My great-grandfather, Big Daddy, sold it along with my Mam's famous fried apple pies in his small store that stood next to our house until it burned long before I was born.

Everyone in town called Big Daddy's store "King's Paradise". I always thought it was a strange name for a store, but one day Momma explained prohibition and the great depression to me, and after that, it made perfect sense. Big Daddy was what you now call an entrepreneur, but there were other names for him too: one was bootlegger, another was rum runner and my favorite was moon-shiner, because I love the moon.

King's Paradise stood just a stone's throw from the big old house that Big Daddy and Mam lived in since the beginning of time; so Mam and Big Daddy's "home place" as they call it, also came to be known as King's Paradise. But I am getting away from the main point: tomorrow is a special day.

I suppose I should finish with the naming of Mam and Big Daddy's children so you are not totally confused when I say their names later. First, there is Uncle Birch and of course, his dead twin

Willow. Then there was Uncle Coal, who I never knew because he died in his early twenties in a car accident hauling a load of my Big Daddies "spirits" to Meridian, Mississippi. There is Uncle Jasper; he is a preacher at the Beulah Baptist Church in Hopewell Springs. He is very old now, at least seventy-one, but he still keeps on preaching Sunday after Sunday. For a while, he was a circuit preacher and had four different churches he served. He was at Beulah, Mount Olive, and Friendship and finally Hopewell Springs. But eventually the people of Beulah chipped in and built him a little cabin right next to the cemetery and paid him enough to just stay put in Beulah. I guess they liked him a lot.

I have always been scared to death of Uncle Jasper because we have to go to church and he screams and yells the whole time about hell, fire and damnation. I leave every time thinking I need to be re-baptized. Sugar Lea tells me not to worry, that's why she quit going to church years ago. She said she had been baptized so many times, the last time she saw the face of Jesus as she closed her eyes and was dunked, and He was just shaking His head back and forth as if to say, enough!

In October 1960, a bright fireball fell to the earth in Western Australia. Fragments of this meteor were later recovered, and were found to contain pyroxine, which indicates the meteor was a fragment from the asteroid Vesta, blasted from Vesta's surface in the remote past. It was announced this year that this meteor could positively be connected to Vesta. Symbolically, it appears that Vesta, keeper of the Sacred Fire, sent to Earth a fireball from this fire—and it landed in the country of the Southern Cross, Australia. Vesta, the brightest of the asteroids, sending some of her light to Earth.

—Solarviews.com

Sugar Lea is sometimes a psychic and just knows things Uncle Jasper can never know, even with all his religion in his head.

After Uncle Jasper there is Aunt Ivory, she is an "old maid" and teaches first grade at Hopewell

Springs School. There is only one school in Hopewell Springs, first grade through twelfth. I like Aunt Ivory, but sometimes she seems strange because she talks to herself all the time. She still lives in the big house at King's Paradise, and more or less keeps to herself in her own room under the eaves of the attic. She has about twenty bird feeders nailed to the ledge of her windows and she mostly talks to herself and her birds. She is nice to me, but I think she prefers her cardinals and her wrens.

After Aunt Ivory there is Aunt Topaz. I love Aunt Topaz. She too is an "old maid", which means technically she has never been married, but it is not because no one ever asked. Sugar Lea says Aunt Topaz could have had any man in the whole state of Alabama at any time in her life. She is what we call eccentric. She left Hopewell Springs years ago to become an "actress". And she was a friend of that famous woman, Zelda Fitzgerald—before she married Scott Fitzgerald, the famous writer. Mam let Aunt Topaz basically do what she wanted to do from the time she was born, because that is the way the two of them worked. Aunt Topaz was fearless and Mam was fearful that if she didn't give Aunt Topaz a very long rope she would lose her.

First, Aunt Topaz went to New Orleans. She mingled with Tennessee Williams, the famous playwright and other writers. She claimed Mr. Tennessee wrote her into one of his plays called, *A Streetcar Named Desire*, but Sugar Lea said that was a bald face lie and not to believe a single word she ever said. I took the other road and devoured every word she said; I longed to be just like her when I grow up. She was the most beautiful women on Earth to me. She was in New Orleans a real long time and would send me postcards of the French Quarter and all the pretty architecture, because I love houses. I loved getting those cards; it made me feel so important. That is what I love about Aunt Topaz; she makes everyone feel good and important. I do not think Sugar Lea and Aunt Topaz have ever really gotten along, and for that matter I do not think Aunt Ivory gets along with either one of them, but they all live in our big house, King's Paradise.

At various times I heard stories I think I should not have heard, referring to Aunt Topaz's acting skills. Once I heard the term "dancer" mingled with "actress", so for years I pictured her dressed up in a ballerina outfit, but I realized when I got to be nine there were other kinds of dancers. Anyway, Aunt Topaz has moved back to King's Paradise because she is "middle-aged", but to me she is still beautiful and still inclined to "dramatics" as Sugar Lea likes to say.

Aunt Topaz looks a lot like Elizabeth Taylor or Marilyn Monroe, depending on what her hair color is on any given day. She switches back and forth between black or very blonde peroxide. At one time there was talk that she was going to move to Hollywood in California to be a "stand-in" for Miss Taylor or Miss Monroe, but it never happened. Aunt Topaz has many glamorous pictures of herself where she even made a little beauty mark on her upper lip. Her dyed hair really irritates Sugar Lea, but she does it anyway. I really, really love her and it does not bother me at all that she is eccentric.

Then there is my grandmother, Camellia the second, or as we all call her Sugar Lea. Mam started calling her Sugar Lea right from the start because she said she saved the sweetest for last. My grandmother is sweet. She is also funny, smart, and pretty and the "glue" that has kept King's Paradise together all these years. So now, you know my family, or at least the main people.

Here is my story, and so help me God, it is all true.

Kings Paradise

10:00 P.M., June 19, 1963

I was having a hard time falling asleep. I was too excited to sleep. My bedroom was next door to Mam's room. Big Daddy died thirty years ago while he was hauling boxes of Mam's scuppernong wine from the root house. It was a massive heart attack and the Doctor said he died instantly and felt no pain. It was painful for Mam because she loved him as much that day as she loved him since the first day they met at King's Paradise. I wish I had known Big Daddy; everyone says he was the biggest man they ever saw, and he had the biggest heart of anyone they ever knew.

I loved to sleep close to Mam, because I loved her more than I loved anyone or anything. I could not bear the thought that she was going to be 100. Being 100 seemed like the end of time, the death number. Being rational, I knew anyone surviving 100 had little time left, but Mam was slipping away. Sugar Lea felt Mam was on the edge of Heaven already. Mam would sit upright in bed and see people she had known throughout her life standing at the foot of her bed talking to her about things that had mattered, like had she made the ice cream for the church social, how many calves were born in February (that was important because a calf born after February had a tougher time, don't ask me why), and had she remembered it was Thelma Hubbard's birthday next week. Memories haunted her, though she couldn't even remember who she was on some days.

What a terrible thing to lose your memory. I would sit at her feet most of the day and show her pictures of old times when she was young and laughing. There was one picture my Mother took of Mam when she was chopping off the head of a chicken to make her world famous chicken and dumplings for dinner. She had a smile the size of Texas plastered across her face and I must have shown her that particular picture 100 times to get some kind of reaction from her. Finally, she took it in her hands and studied it as if it was the *Mona Lisa.*

I said, "Look Mam, it's you when you were younger killing a chicken just to make Momma some chicken and dumplings, look how funny you are!"

Mam just kept on studying that picture, laid it across her ample bosom and went to sleep holding it there for the rest of the day. Finally she woke up and looked me straight in the face and said, "Write it all down."

That was all she said, *"Write it all down."*

I took it literally and have been trying to find a way to write this story, which I think is what she meant. I just know in my heart she wanted it to be written down so generations would know about King's Paradise and what took place on the night of June 19, 1963. Mam told me from an early age that we learn from our past mistakes. Hopefully this world will someday learn from the past and correct the injustice that still exists.

I told Sugar Lea what Mam said about writing it all down and she said it was best to just leave her be and not to pay any attention to what she said, but I could not let it go.

It was the last time she really looked into my eyes and said something! I could not just let it be, I wanted her back the way she was. I wanted us all back the way we were. So I figured I would write it all down for Mam.

So here goes my story and I suppose it is the story of all the women from King's Paradise, and ultimately it is the story of the end of Mam's life at King's Paradise.

THE PARTY OF TWO

I am going to start with the end because that is where the story really begins. It is funny that on this night I learned the true beginning also.

We were all in a stew over the party. There was food to prepare and flowers to arrange, because ever Southern woman knows a home isn't suitably appointed until there are enough flower arrangements scattered about to make it look like a viewing for a funeral. There were vegetables to pick, eggs to gather, cows to milk and homemade wine to decant so the sediment wouldn't cloud the glasses when it poured. There was so much to do just to get through one ordinary day at King's

Paradise, but to have a party for 200 people was something big.

I spent the day helping Sugar Lea, Aunt Ivory, Aunt Topaz and various other kin in the kitchen. Momma offered to have the entire party catered from the *Piggly Wiggly* Delicatessen but Sugar Lea had a fit and said, "Absolutely not!" It made Momma mad so she stayed in her room grading papers all day, even though we really could have used an extra hand.

Momma was changing. There was a movement just starting out at the University called the "Woman's Movement," most of us at King's Paradise were in the dark as to what that actually meant. Momma had become "haughty," according to Sugar Lea. "Reckless" and "Irreverent" were other adjectives screamed back and forth between their rooms in passing. Momma, being a Professor at the University, was also actively involved in the Civil Rights movement sweeping across the State like a comet off track heading for a crash if not stopped in time. Mississippi had seen so much bloodshed already because of the movement and

Alabama was sure to see its own share of bloodshed before too long. Our family was what you could call compassionate toward the Negroes in our town.

Besides Mam, Sugar Lea and my aunts, I was practically raised since birth by Ada Maude, our own personal maid. She was more than a maid to us she was like family. Her momma and daddy lived in a small little house on the edge of the big woods that bordered our pastures. Ada Maude did housework for Mam since I can remember. She had no formal education, but Mam taught her to read and write and she spent a good deal of her time now writing poetry, and with Mam's help she wrote sermons to Dr. Martin Luther King. It is hard to say exactly how old she is because she still looks the same as she did to me when I first remember seeing her small gold colored eyes darting like drunken snails across her face. She is a small black woman with high Indian cheekbones, which make her look more Indian than Negro, but Mam says she is full Negro, so I guess she is. She is very religious, does not drink anything stronger that the pot licker that boils down from the ever-present pot of turnip greens she keeps simmering on her wood stove. She sustains herself on turnip greens, cornbread and buttermilk for every meal, and she says it is the reason she is still alive.

Her face is lineless, yet her hands have the age of wisdom and time marked across the top of her palms like an aged watch. I love Ada Maude just as much as I love Mam, Sugar Lea and my assorted aunts, and of course Momma, but Ada Maude is different. Her love is timeless and effortless. She lets me get away with most anything I care to do. And she has even let me try her snuff, which she keeps in her bottom lip, even when she sleeps at night. It made me awfully sick and I vomited one whole afternoon, but I stayed hidden in Ada Maude's room next to the kitchen where she has lived for the past twenty years or so. She stood over me and fanned me with a cardboard picture of Dr. Martin Luther King she got from one of her cousins who lived in town. Emblazoned across the face of the fan was a picture of Martin Luther

King holding the hand of Jesus with a giant rainbow circling their heads like a halo. The words,

> *Even though we face the difficulties of today and tomorrow, I still have a dream. I have a dream that one day this nation will rise up and live out the true meaning of its creed: "We hold these truths to be self-evident, that all men are created equal."*
>
> —Dr. Martin Luther King, Jr.

were printed on the other side of the fan; Ada Maude made me spend one entire afternoon helping her to memorize them. She loved Dr. King and had instilled in me a love for him, I suppose.

"Ada Maude, you ever wish you knew Dr. King, in real life I mean."

"I'll have you know I met him on two occasions when I was younger, and I knows his wife Coretta, and I even knows Coretta's sweet Mother, Berniece McMurray Scott… Oh chile, there are secrets and stories I wish I could tell you, tell someone, but your mother and your grandmother would beat me with a whip if I ever told you all the secrets that rest in my bosom. I keep them close to my heart so I will never forget them. Oh Lawd Almighty, I wish I could forget them; they don't do me no good and no good would come if they were known, but it might make a big change if they were brought to light," Ada Maude said as she became restless and picked up a quilt that needed mending, fumbling with the broken stitches.

"Ada Maude, you can tell me, I promise on Mam's heart, I swear even. I won't tell nobody a word, you can trust me, and I won't even tell Aunt Topaz," I said in all earnest.

Ada Maude laughed her deep rich laugh that told me Aunt Topaz already knew this secret. Aunt Topaz had a way of knowing everything, and if she couldn't get a secret out of you the first time she needled and whittled away at you until you had to give in just to get away from the scent of her Jungle Gardenia, which she would douse on herself heavier and heavier until anyone would become vulnerable and weakened with the scent, and soon enough she would have her story. She was a collector of stories and secrets, the gatekeeper to our family's skeletons and sorrows alike.

"You already know your Aunt Topaz done got it out of me before I have to tell you, but she done swore her soul to this family, and I believe her because she was the one who tolt me how big this secret was, and how it might be best kept between as few people as possible. Of course them other people know the truth, and I am talking about them big, high-mighty people. You could say this secret is the biggest secret under God's sky now. I think you could know this secret, because God only knows if I am called home, or Topaz, we talked about telling you, as a matter of fact, just so the secret will not die when we pass on."

"Okay then if Aunt Topaz thinks I can handle this big secret why not tell me now?" I asked swinging my arms back and forth in a desperate motion of urgency.

"I think I needs to talk to Topaz first, where is that girl now."

"Last time I saw her was after breakfast, you know before I took in the snuff and got so sick. Do you think she can smell it on my breath?'

"Lawd no. She probably been smoking all day anyway and reading some of her white trash books, that girl won't never change. Go find her and bring her here, don't tell her I tolt you anything about the secret; we'll tell you together, because my mind is not as sharp as it once was. Lawd knows I want to get the facts straight… Go on now, find her and let me rest my eyes a spell while you do, and bring me back a piece of that sweet potato pie from the pie case when you come back."

I raced from the room and ran in the direction of the side porch where Momma and Aunt Topaz were allowed to smoke, as long as they put their cigarette butts in an old coffee can filled with lavender as fine and pure as purple rice. Aunt Topaz was seated in the corner, folded into a worn wicker rocker, which had seen better days, with one of her so called white trash books, only it was

William Faulkner; Ada Maude considered anything vulgar and white trash if it wasn't the Bible. Aunt Topaz was engrossed in the book and didn't notice me standing in the doorway. I studied her face for a few minutes and realized she was getting old like all the women at King's Paradise. Even me, for only this morning I noticed the first hairs growing on my legs. Her hair was in need of a dye job; it was teetering on black roots, which had specks of gray throughout, and golden ends which looked fried and held in place by hair salve. She had on red lipstick with a cigarette, unlit, clenched in her mouth, making the lines around her mouth all the more noticeable and pinched. I coughed to get her attention.

"Hey, Baby girl come over here and give me a hug, I need one, I have just been through the most awful ordeal with one of Mr. Faulkner's characters, want to hear about it?" I knew better than to say yes, for Aunt Topaz often mixed up reality with any of her literary heroines or heroes. She had a special affinity for Faulkner; she claimed she had met him several times when she lived in New

Orleans or Biloxi. Sugar Lea said they were all made up lies to impress, and she said no one at King's Paradise gave a care about Mr. Faulkner or Aunt Topaz's fantasies, for who had time for fantasies when there was a real world which needed constant tending just like a garden or the rearing of a child, neither of which Aunt Topaz had ever been inclined to try.

"Not now Aunt Topaz, Ada Maude sent me to fetch you to her room right now, she said it is important. You go on, I got to get her a piece of sweet potato pie. Want a piece for yourself and a cup of coffee?" I asked her, and by the time I finish I see she is intrigued at the thought of what Ada Maude wants from her.

"Yes sweetheart, bring me a piece too, and would you find Uncle Jack and pour three fingers into my coffee, by now it is probably as strong as river silt and needs some cutting. You know I never eat dairy products or sugar, to keep my figure in shape, so just load it up with Uncle Jack. On second thought, skip the coffee and just pour me a full cup of Uncle Jack, if there is enough in the bottle, and don't tell your grandmother," She said, as she turned her back to me heading in the direction of Ada Maude's room.

I opened the cupboard where the "cooking alcohol" was held and found half a bottle of Uncle Jack. Jack was also hidden in the upstairs linen closet in case anyone suffered a bad case of insomnia on any given night; there seemed to be an epidemic of insomnia in our household. I sliced two pieces of the pie with the silver pie server and laid out a pretty tray with the two pieces, Ada Maude's black coffee and the brown mug of Aunt Topaz's afternoon tonic. I slipped Uncle Jack back into his spot in the cupboard, put away the pie, closed all the doors on the cupboards and walked slowly back in the direction of Ada Maude's room. The door was ajar and I could hear Aunt Topaz raising her voice in a gentle roar, scolding Ada Maude for something. I guessed it had to do with the secret I was about to learn. I knew from experience that even though Aunt Topaz might be reluctant to talk at the beginning, the more sips she had of her Uncle Jack the more her tongue would loosen and make it more and more pliable and eager to join in the conversation, divulging the secret with Ada Maude. I couldn't wait. I couldn't imagine what it could be. Or who it could be about. I secretly hoped it was about my mother or perhaps my daddy, but I knew that was a taboo secret, which I would never know the truth about.

"I'm back!" I announced as I trotted in with the tray and the drinks.

"Well darling you are a real lady, look at the presentation of this wonderful afternoon tea," Aunt Topaz said standing to take the tray from me, she made room for it on the end of Ada Maude's bed, for her room was small and there wasn't a place cleaned off on the only table next to her bed. There were two straight back rocking chairs occupied by Ada Maude and Aunt Topaz, so I curled myself up and sat on the floor at their feet. Aunt Topaz reached for her mug and drained it in one enormous gulp; she gave a small belch, excused herself, and offered me her piece of pie, which I took out of duty. Ada Maude left her pie and coffee untouched, even when I offered to hand them to her. She had tears rolling down her face and I feared Aunt Topaz had frightened her or scared her regarding the mysterious secret. Aunt Topaz spoke first. She licked her lips and her tongue circled the remains of Uncle Jack from the perimeters of her mouth, her lipstick became smudged and bled onto her teeth; I tried not to stare at her mouth while she talked and focused on the quilt in Ada Maude's lap she had started to repair. Aunt Topaz had obviously already been partaking of Uncle Jack long before she had her cup with us for her speech was slightly slurred like it became when she over-imbibed.

"Well, Junie, it seems Ada Maude thinks you are ready to become the third generation of our family to learn a very dangerous and highly secretive piece of information, which has implications all the way to the seat of our highest place of government. I for one do not think you are old enough or wise enough to know this secret; however, Ada Maude makes a very good point in saying that this secret should never die, and none of us knows when our Lord will take us home to be with him… So I suppose it may be time to tell you. You do know we are in the midst of the greatest war our nation has seen since the great Civil War which divided our great states don't you dear?"

"Yessam, if you are meaning the Civil rights war."

"Exactly my dear!" Aunt Topaz exclaimed.

"Well honey, it pains me to tell you that it wasn't so very long ago that our family had slaves who worked the land here at King's Paradise, although they weren't technically slaves—they were our workers who kept things running for Big Daddy and Mam to build up their fortune which has left us all comfortable to our dying days. Of course Ada Maude was a vital part of our family being shaped into what it is today, one of the finest families in the history of Hopewell Springs and all the surrounding counties. Why we have had Civil War Generals in our family and we even harken back to the Revolutionary War when this land was bequeathed to Big Daddy's ancestors as part of a war land grant. None of this could have happened without slavery. Not that I have ever condoned it, nor accepted it as a means to an end, but nonetheless, we are at fault by our birthright as white Southerners to share in the guilt and shame of what we did to so many of the poor slaves descended from Kings Paradise and beyond." Aunt Topaz was inclined to theatrics and loved an audience more than anyone I knew, so I clapped when she finished and looked to Ada Maude with a knowing look. She too made a feeble attempt to applaud, though I knew her heart wasn't in it. Mine either, I just knew how to handle Aunt Topaz.

"Well, I will attempt to tell the story Ada Maude has alluded to, and she will of course from time to time help me clarify details for there are many in this story, although by its own merit it is a simple story, given the circumstances that surround it. So I shall begin."

THE SECRET

Aunt Topaz began to read from yellowed papers she pulled from the pocket of her bathrobe, even though it was long past afternoon, the robe was stained with coffee and another brown liquid, which I knew to be Uncle Jack, and it reeked of alcohol and her fragrance of choice, Jungle Gardenia. She stood poised and regal and could have been standing in the spotlight of a vast auditorium giving the performance of her life. She began reciting from memory, yet clinging to the paper as if it were the holy gospel, looking at it now and then to validate her performance.

Thomas Jefferson Taylor II, the father of little Lady Bird, was born 29 August, 1874, in Autauga County. General store owner; cotton planter; land owner; a sharecropper's son who became a wealthy businessman and the owner of fifteen thousand acres of cotton and two general stores when he moved to Texas after leaving Alabama. There isn't much known about his early time in Alabama, but he was a big, stout man and he hated the Negroes. In later years Miss Lady Bird would say about her father, "My father was a very strong character, to put it mildly, he lived by his own rules." It was really a feudal way of life. Mr. Taylor died 22 October, 1960 in Marshall, Texas; turning his store profits into real estate, he owned some twelve thousand acres of cotton, perhaps the largest landowner in Harrison County, Texas; he donated nearly four hundred acres of property, some two-thirds of the total, to the state and it became Caddo Lake State Park; he also owned the property on which the Longhorn Army Ammunition Plant was built during World War II.

Lady Bird's mother, Miss Minnie Pattillo, was born 16 May, 1874 in probably Billingsly, Alabama. She was from a gentile family of English and Scottish descent. The family name was Pattillo. Likely because Mexico borders her later native Texas, it had been mistakenly published in some accounts that her mother's family was of Spanish ancestry. In fact, the origin of the name is "Pittillo" and her first American ancestor was James Pittillo of Bristol Parish, Virginia. The family emigrated from Scotland.

Miss Minnie married Thomas J. Taylor in Autauga County, Alabama on 28 November, 1900; died 4 September 1918; Some sources claim a date death of 14 September; Mrs. Johnson recalls the dismay of relatives at the tombstone date error. "Forgetful of self she lived entirely for others" is the epitaph. The town of birth is not known but she did live her early life in Billingsly, Alabama.

Miss Lady Bird was the third of three children; two brothers, Thomas Jefferson Taylor, Jr. born 20 October 1901 and died 1 November 1959,

> *and Antonio "Tony" J. Taylor born 29 August, 1904 and he is still alive.*

Aunt Topaz stopped reading and started a rambling soliloquy, "Ada Maude remembers Miss Lady Bird being small in stature, with brilliant brown hair and sad brown eyes; yet she was a pretty girl, which is how she got the name 'Lady Bird'."

> *Her given name was Claudia Alta, named after her uncle Claude, "Lady Bird" was given by her maid because she declared she was "as pretty as a Lady Bird".*

Aunt Topaz paused to light up one of her Winston's, "Ada Maude when was the first time you met Miss Effie?"

"Well, best I can remember I was 'bout foteen, cause that was the year my momma died and Miss Effie heard 'bout my momma dying and knewed I didn't have no other place to go, so I say foteen was 'bout right," Ada Maude said rocking back and forth in her maple rocking chair, the steady click clack almost pulling me into a deep sleep, but I appeared interested in what Aunt Topaz had to say nonetheless. I was after all going to be privy to a real secret.

Aunt Topaz continued reading.

Lady Bird's mother was the former Minnie Lee Pattillo, an opera lover who felt out of place in Karnack, Texas.

"Can you blame her for that? Imagine going to live in such a God forsaken place as Texas; why, you might as well go straight to hell. Sorry Ada Maude."

Miss Minnie was often in poor emotional and physical health. When Lady Bird was five years old, Minnie, while pregnant, fell down a flight of stairs and died of complications after miscarrying.

"Can you imagine? It wouldn't surprise me one bit if old man Taylor pushed her to her death so he could gain her wealth."

Mam remembers Miss Minnie as a tall, eccentric woman who liked to wear long white dresses and heavy veils, and liked to scandalize people for miles around by entertaining Negroes in her home.

"We can sure vouch for that, can't we Ada Maude?"

She once started writing a book about Negro religious practices, called "Bio Baptism".

"Ada Maude concurs, we have no idea what 'Bio Baptism' means, but that was the way Miss Minnie's mind worked, she was so intelligent and scholarly, so the Lord only knows what the hell that means."

Her unreconstructed husband, however, tended to see blacks as hewers of wood and drawers of water. He insisted all the Negroes call him "Boss Man".

"All talk of that ne'er-do-well will come when Ada Maude's tells her tale."

Lady Bird visited Alabama every summer until she was a young woman. She is claimed to have said, "Until I was about 20, summertime always meant Alabama to me. With Aunt Effie we would board the train in Marshall and ride to the part of the world that meant watermelon cuttings, picnics at the creek, and a lot of company every Sunday." According to Lady Bird, her aunt Effie, "opened my spirit to beauty, but she neglected to give me any insight into the practical matters a girl should know about, such as how to dress or choose one's friends or learning to dance."

"Mam says Lady Bird was a shy and quiet girl who spent much of her youth alone in the outdoors."

"People always look back at it now and assume I was lonely," she once said about her childhood, "to me I definitely was not, I spent a lot of time just walking and fishing and swimming." She developed her lifelong love of the environment as a child growing up in the tall hardwoods and pine and vast woodlands and swamps of Alabama.

"What in God's name does all this have to do with an important secret?" I asked Aunt Topaz as she kept the papers in her lap and her glasses pushed onto the tip of her nose like an old maid school teacher.

"Darling, we're getting to the secret, but I took considerable time and trouble to write this all down for future generations, so the real secret will have validity and not be taken as some back woods rumor. Be patient, I'm getting to the secret, but it will be told from memory by Ada Maude. Honey, we could never, and I mean never, write down *the* secret. Why our very lives could all be in danger, especially the life of your daddy." Upon saying the name "Daddy", she grasped her hands across her mouth and realized she said the wrong thing. I did not move or wince or even pretend I heard her, for now I knew my daddy was alive and somehow this secret, whatever it was, had something to do him. MY DADDY WAS ALIVE! I suddenly felt happy and jubilant and wanted to jump for joy on Ada Maude's neatly made bed; although I knew that was rule number one in our house, once a bed was made for the day there was no lying across it. It was considered bad luck, even an omen of an impending death within our house. Still, I wanted to jump for joy.

"Well I don't care to hear any more of this history about a family I don't even know," I said defiantly.

"What in God's name do you mean? I am talking about Our Second Lady, the Second Lady of the United States of America. Mrs. Lyndon Baines Johnson!" She exclaimed, as if I were a total disgrace and moron.

"Okay, go on, but I want to get to the good part."

"In due time darling, in due time," She finished saying.

She pushed her hair off her head and resumed talking in her theatrical voice which always had a twinge of an English accent. It sent Sugar Lea through the roof when Aunt Topaz started talking with an English accent.

When Mrs. Johnson was only five years old, her mother died and her aunt, Effie Patillo, who never married, moved to Texas to care for the child. Ada Maude was one of the few coloreds to stay in the big house when Miss Effie moved to Texas, because even if there weren't meals and parties to plan, the house needed caring for, as all Southern houses of distinction do.

They would return to Alabama each summer to live in the house and spend all summer long on the large Verandah that encircled the house. Mam, who was only a few years older than Miss Effie, was Miss Eiffie's best friend. They were intellectuals and everyone knew they would chose to sympathize with the Negro causes of freedom and the right to vote.

Big Daddy would accompany Mam to the Patillo's at least every other week where there were grand parties. Mam and Miss Effie were both very bright and loved to read and exchanged many hours of conversation on things of the world and wonders of the universe.

Miss Effie's brother Claude…

"You know, who little Lady Bird, *Claudia Alta*, was named after…"

Claude was very eccentric and was often seen sun bathing in the nude on top of the porch.

"Can you imagine in those days! Not that I haven't done it myself on many occasions right here at King's Paradise. Anyway…"

There is a tale told that one day Ivory…

"Our Ivory, can you imagine?"

Ivory was called by Miss Effie to come help clip back the roses.

"Ivory as we all know has always had the green thumb in this family. And Ivory was always a bit scared to go to the Patillo house because she was a straight as an arrow, even as a child, and the thought of going to an eccentric person's house scared the hell out of her. Anyway…"

Uncle Claude was a health food fanatic and used to sunbathe nude on the balcony claiming it would draw the poison from your innards and give you a long life. Ivory was tending the roses near the cemetery behind the house when Mr. Claude called out to her, "Little girl! Don't look up here. I'm nekkid as a jaybird." She did of course look up and was shocked.

"I'd say that's why Ivory has remained celibate to this day; seeing his penis, excuse my vulgarity, but seeing it must have shocked her to death. She never went back there to tend roses or even to parties."

There are many people who claim Mr. Claude has numerous families of black children, called Mullatos.

"You can even go check the records at the courthouse and they are there, sure enough, listed on the registers as full citizens."

The Patillo family, according to Mam, was one that, "stuck close together." She visited them at the Autauga County plantation many, many times and was impressed by their friendly, almost clannish, attitude toward each other.

"Only One Left now; they are all gone," Aunt Topaz said sadly, "so far as I know, only the child is left. And they were wonderful people; they were good Christian people."

"What child is left?" I asked.

"Why, Lady Bird." Aunt Topaz said.

"But she isn't a child any longer."

"Oh well, let's not be too technical. You're correct; she is no longer a child."

Aunt Topaz continued.

Lady Bird was baptized at age five in the Methodist faith of her father; she later became Episcopalian. And she and Mam would take turns putting flowers in the church on Sunday mornings. After church, Miss Effie would throw a big lunch and that is how Ada Maude became such a famous cook in the county.

One night there was a heavenly party given at the home of Miss Effie and Mr. Claude on a Saturday, in honor of Miss Somebody-I-Can't-Remember.

"I was invited, I believe the entire county was invited, white folks and Negroes alike, but of course when many of the white folks got wind of the fact Miss Effie had invited the Negroes there were only a few people who actually showed up. The whites stayed away on account of the Negroes and the Negroes stayed away on account that they knew their place; and I do not say this disparagingly at all, I say it because that was the way things were then. Come to think of it, it is the same way now."

The house was beautifully decorated with fauna and ferns from the gardens of the house. The time was spent in games and amusements of all kinds until supper, when delightful refreshments were served in the tastily decorated dining hall. Through the kindness of the host and hostess, the occasion was made one to be long remembered by the lucky people present.

After supper games of all kinds were played. A beautiful book was won by Mam, which I believe she still owns as a prize for pinning the elephant's trunk in the proper place while blindfolded. A cake walk followed next, the judges declared the winners to be Mam and Big Daddy. Ada Maude was there also, helping out with the food and the clearing of tables.

Mam came across some of the letters she had shared with Miss Effie—even though it was only ten miles away from King's Paradise, they still corresponded by mail. Mam said one day, "I bundled them up and mailed them to Mrs. Johnson in Washington." Some weeks later, Mam received the nicest letter from Mrs. Johnson. "It was a personal letter, written in long-hand, and she thanked me for the letters, saying they contained much information about the Patillo family she didn't know before."

Mam recalls Lady Bird as being outgoing and bubbly, a unique person, real down to earth.

"I know all this, you just keep repeating yourself," I said, growing more and more impatient, "get to the point or you can keep your damn secret. I'm tired of all this history. I get enough history in school."

"Well okay, have it your way. But you better watch your mouth young lady, or I'll haul your butt to the kitchen and give you a taste of lye soap on that smart tongue of yours!" Aunt Topaz said. I for one think she was glad for the break because it was time for her three fingers of Uncle Jack; and sure enough, she excused herself from the room with her brown mug and said she had to refresh her lipstick, that all the talking had made her mouth dry too.

I closed my eyes and prayed to God that the secret had something to do with my Daddy; that I was finally going to know the truth about my Daddy. Ada Maude seemed quiet and subdued and tired, but she put another plug of her snuff under her lip and prepared to tell me the real secret. After a few minutes, Aunt Topaz reentered the room, sure enough with her mouth all red and glossy and her little brown mug held tightly in her hand.

"Okay Ada Maude, I suppose it is up to you to divulge the secret to our little Miss Junebug. But let me say a word before you do, we must take a blood vow that it never leaves this room. Never! Junie, when the time comes you can choose a blood relative to tell the secret, but only when you trust that person to keep it a secret. I got a big old sewing needle here and we are all going to prick our fingers and let our blood meld together, and that will be our blood secret."

"What in God's holy name are you talking about Topaz Irene Cribbs?" Ada Maude yelled across to Aunt Topaz.

"It's just a ceremony, so we all know how important this secret is and how we cannot divulge any of it for fear our very lives may be in danger. Come on Ada Maude, let's do it."

Ada Maude gave in to the blood pricking and we all held our middle fingers together for a few seconds until our blood became a mix of generations of strong women—my first thought, and a generation of slightly mad women—my second.

Ada Maude sat up straight in her rocking chair, and for the first time in years she seemed to look younger, and had a almost childlike quality to her. She spit the plug of tobacco into the coffee can she kept as a spitoon and cleared her throat. Then she spoke, trying her best to use the good grammar Mam taught her to use, "Well, now that

Topaz has introduced you to the Patillo family, I reckon it's my time to tell you the secret, which has to do with the Patillo family, so to speak. Like Topaz said, I was nearly 14 when I went to live with the Patillos. They had some real nice little cabins in the back of the house for us workers to stay in. We even had wood floors and real beds to sleep in. Miss Effie, she was a good Christian woman, and like her sister Miss Minnie, who was the mother of little Lady Bird, she had her own kind of eccentric ways about her. She paid us once a week for our jobs and let us have Sunday's off to worship at our own churches, and on rainy days she gave the truck keys to Big Jack, and we would all pile into the cab of the truck and make our way to church. Those were some happy days, mainly 'cause Miss Effie and Miss Minnie—God rest her poor soul—loved to have parties and entertain. It was nothing to see white folks mingling with black folks or even Mulatoos, which populated the county. It was a known fact there were many Mulatoo Patillos in our community, and they had many of the same names as the white Patillos. I knew at least five named Minne. Oh Lawd, Miss Minnie, she was such a fine Christian woman, but that husband of hers was a no-count, a ne'er-do-well straight from the bowels of hell itself.

"When Miss Minnie died and Miss Effie came back during the summers to raise Lady Bird, most of the colored girls would quit working for Miss Effie and Mr. Claude. I know they knew why too, 'cause old man Taylor loved to have his pick of the colored girls at the farm or close by it. The men folk was too scared of him to do anything about it, 'cause he carried a shotgun with him everywhere he went, and it was a known fact he hanged at least three or four of the men who tried to stop him from his ways.

"The last summer Miss Effie and Miss Lady Bird come to stay, old man Taylor was there too. He had missed a few summers in between on account of all the half-white babies he fathered all over the community, and the Episcopalian preacher gone to him and asked him to heal himself from his evil ways and take responsibility and pay for those babies and help the mothers. He just stayed away, but that last summer proved to be the last time he would put harm on any woman from town, and her name was Berniece McMurray. Berniece was as purty as a girl could be, and she looked almost white, except for her hair. Berneice must have been about 21 years old. She was a strong girl, in charge of running the house when Miss Effie was away. I saw how men looked at her. I was almost 44 by then and was still developing myself and still caught the eye of some men, even though I was promised to Big Jack. Big Jack was determined, before we would marry, he would own his own house and his own truck. It was the year before Willow was born. Mam thinks Willow's slow mind came for me birthing her in my middle age, but I can't think of that now. I was scared to death of Mr. Taylor, but he knew better than lay a hand on me 'cause he would have had Mam or Big Jack to deal with."

"But Ada Maude, I thought you grew up at King's Paradise this entire time. Didn't you grew up here?" I asked exploringly, confused.

"Me and Big Jack moved into the house behind King's Paradise, the little house I was born in, the last year of joy at the Patillo place, 1928. And we lived there and was happy until my man, Big Jack Brown, died from a heart dropsy in 1940. Then Mam had me move into the house and be the housekeeper at King's Paradise. This is my home, and this room is my own piece of heaven right here on earth," She said brushing a tear from her cloudy yellow eyes.

Ada Maude continued, "One night just before darkness fell, I heard the loudest scream and I just kept on running in the direction of the scream and there I found Berneice laying in some tall grass just outside the fence of the graveyard. I didn't even have to ask her what happened. She crawled into my arms and I held onto her and let her cry and get it out of her. She was bloodied up and her dress was torn down the front like a dog had mauled her, and I guess you might say a dog had mauled her, that god-damned Thomas Jefferson Taylor. He weren't nowhere to be found. I run up to the house to tell Miss Effie what he done and she told me he would be on the first train back to Texas by day light; and I guess he was cause we never saw him again after that day. It was a hot night about the end of July, getting on time for Miss Effie and Miss Lady Bird to leave, 'cause Miss Lady Bird, she was getting to be a social girl in her own right; She was near on 15. She was still a shy, quiet child who seemed to be scared of her own shadow, and we all knews she was scared to death of that daddy she had. Looking back I think Miss Minnie, Lord bless her soul, must have had the same feelings about old man Taylor; no telling how many chuldren he done made on this earth. Miss Minnie must had told Miss Effie, if anything ever happen to her that she take care of Miss Lady Bird.

"Berneice stayed with us that night, Miss Effie had Big Jack drove over to her house and told her husband, Mr. Obe, that she had gotten the heat dropsy during the day picking the garden, and she would return the next day. Berneice had another girl at home, a purdy little girl named Edythe and it was the first time Berneice had been away from

Edythe, but she knew better than to go home and let Obe see her in her condition. Miss Effie and me washed her in the big washing tub with warm water, and Miss Effie herself put salve on her scratches and bruises and gave her a sleeping tonic, and she even let me sleep with her myself. It was a restless night for both of us. All night long all Berniece prayed was that the seed had not planted itself in her womb and there would be no baby from this horrible attack from Mr. Taylor.

"After a few weeks, it came time for Miss Effie and Miss Lady Bird to leave and go back to Texas, and during that time Miss Effie took good care of Berneice and let her have light duties around the house like dusting the rooms and shelling peas or butter beans and putting up the vegetables rather than the picking of them. But a woman knows what a woman knows, and it wasn't more than two weeks that Berneice didn't get her blood and we all knew the seed had taken and that she was carrying the baby of old man Taylor. After Miss Effie and Miss Lady Bird left, Berneice knew in her heart she had to tell Obe what happened, and that she was most likely carrying the child of old man Taylor. Obe was mad and angry and blamed her for a few days, but it wasn't her fault God made her so beautiful; just like it wasn't her fault she happened to be alone and attacked by old man Taylor that night in late July. By mid October Berneice's belly was as big and as round as the Harvest Moon, but she was happy knowing she was going to have another chile, cause she was a natural mother.

"Little Coretta Scott was born in the early morning hours of April 27, 1927, almost nine months to the day she was attacked by old man Taylor. She was a purdy baby and Berneice told me the day she was born she was going to amount to something special in the world, something real special 'cause God owed her that. Yes, God owed her that for being conceived in such a violent way.

"Miss Effie and Miss Lady Bird came back to Alabama around the first of May, and Berneice only took a few days off of work on account of they needed the money. Miss Lady Bird was often found in the kitchen looking into the cradle at Coretta, and all summer long she grew to be the caretaker for little Coretta. She begged Miss Effie to buy one of those fancy prams, and Miss Lady Bird would put little Coretta in the pram and push her all over the grounds and show her flowers and would even tell her the names of the trees and such. She read to her, and was the first person little Coretta gave a real smile to. It must have been mighty painful for Berneice to see how Miss Lady Bird doted on Coretta, but why wouldn't she? She was her unlikely sister."

Ada Maude fell back into the rocker and asked me to give her a plug of her tobacco and would I mind going to fetch her a glass of water. When I came back, Aunt Topaz and Ada Maude both had tears standing in their eyes and were as quiet as church mouses. I handed Ada Maude her water.

"Well, I know the secret is that old man Taylor had a daughter with a colored woman, but why is this such a big secret?" I asked, still trying to understand the meaning of the story.

Aunt Topaz reached for Ada Maude's fan, the fan with the picture of Dr. King on it. Then she said something I will never forget until my dying day, "because Junie, little Coretta is the wife of this great man!" She held the face on the fan of Dr. King right up to my nose, "and Miss Lady Bird is the wife of the Vice President of the United States, Mr. Lyndon Baines Johnson."

I fled the room looking for a place to store my secret, for I knew it wasn't right that I should be privy to such information at my age. It didn't seem appropriate. I ran and ran and ran until I found myself knee deep in the hay pasture and I threw my secret heaven bound hoping it would find it's way to the Southern Cross, where it belonged until the time for me to reclaim it. And pass it on.

Ada Maude's little cabin, where she was born, is still standing behind the big house, but the kudzu has consumed it like a hungry lion and it looks like an alien monster during the summer. In the winter, I walk with Ada Maude to the cabin; we push aside the dead kudzu which looks like a spoiled cocoon and we open the small wooden door, and everything is as it was when she was conceived and born. She does not say much about her life; I think there is something painful about her life. I know she had a daughter named Willow, just like my dead great-aunt, who died when she was around eighteen. Willow Fern was her name and she is buried in the colored cemetery across town. Sometimes Momma drives her there to put flowers on Willow's grave. When they come back from visiting her grave Ada Maude and Momma are both red-eyed, take to their beds, and spend the rest of the day crying and moaning. Momma never knew Willow, but the way she carries on with grief is tragic, especially when there is not another human being I know of who would cause her to weep.

"Ada Maude," I said while she was fanning me with the picture of Dr. King, "Why do you suppose Governor Wallace hates you and all the other Negroes so much, and why can't he get along with ya'll? You've never done anything to hurt him or any other white man."

"Oh Lawd Jesus. Honey Baby, it ain't the color of the skin that causes hate to swell up and kill, the devil creeps into the soul of a man when he drinks liquor, that makes him fight and kill. Mans been killing each other since the beginning of time when the devil was set free so mans will kill until the end of time, when Jesus in His majesty comes on home to save us all from hate; it's just hate, plain and simple, hate and ignorance.

"Honey Baby, did you ever see that confederate sword your Mam keeps under her bed?"

I nodded yes because I had held it on many occasions, supervised by Mam of course. It was the sword of her Uncle who had fought with General Lee at Appomattox during the Civil War. It was a curious thing to hold, knowing a weapon so small signified so much, knowing a father, a son, perhaps even a child had lost their life to a cold blade of steel.

"Child, that sword is a remembrance for us all. Hate is born of small things. That war is still being fought now even as we sit here in another century. All we want is our freedom; yes Honey Chile, just our freedom to say and do as we please." Ada Maude had big fat tears rolling off the hollowness of her cheeks and I wanted to catch them and hold her tears like quicksilver, but they were not my tears to hold. I was white and privileged; she was black and still hopeless, and—even after all those years—still fighting a civil war.

She had me read the *Tuskaloosa Times* to her every evening after I finished my chores and homework; lately it was full of Civil Rights news.

Our Governor, George C. Wallace stirred up a hornet's nest by refusing to let two Negro students enter the school only last week. We all packed into Sugar Lea's big ol' Lincoln Continental and drove to the campus on the evening before the event, June 10, 1963, to hear Governor Wallace speak about the horrors of allowing Negroes to attend white colleges. Ada Maude refused to go, but packed us a big basket of fried chicken and cornbread to eat while we made the journey.

Governor Wallace called a rally of all "Christian white men and ladies" to converge across the lush lawns that held the University together by its eternal beauty. Thousands of good white Christian men and the like filled the lawn, trampling on the tender ferns and assorted fauna, and to the left stood a straggly number of Kennedy's men standing in their rumpled shirts and little ties, looking like a group of aliens that had landed in the land of cotton where all is not forgotten. There must have been at least three hundred state troopers; Sugar Lea and Papa were outraged by Governor Wallace's actions and for one night, we all seem united.

Momma was arrested for protesting against the atrocities of Governor Wallace and the actions he had taken against humanity, because she had a poster that accidentally flew out of her hands and hit a state trooper in the face. It made him so mad he yanked Momma out of the crowd and hand-cuffed her on the spot. I didn't actually see her being hand-cuffed, but Ada Maude and Sugar Lea said she was brave for standing up for her rights; everyone made a big deal out of it. Sugar Lea had to pick up Momma from the Tuskaloosa county jailhouse at ten o'clock that night; Papa made her go by herself, because he said if he went he might be inclined to carry his shotgun and show them all what true justice was about. I begged Sugar Lea to let me go, but she was firm in her objection and let me sleep in the bed with Mam that night to make up for not being allowed to go to Tuskaloosa.

Things seemed better for a few days after Momma's arrest. We all sat huddled around our black and white television screen for days watching state troopers and federal marshals keep the peace on campus. Momma was finally able to return to school to teach, but she was given a stern talking-to by the University President, Dr. Frank Rose, about her strong beliefs. But what could he do? Momma was his only astronomer, and she knew the sky and stars like no one else.

For days she sequestered herself inside her small observatory and took comfort in searching the heavens for the Southern Cross. I felt sorry for Momma, but she would not let anyone get close to her and love her. Not even me, her own daughter. I felt sorry for me too, but I kept it in and watched for the Southern Cross from my own telescope that I kept hanging so precariously out of my bedroom window. It gave me hope that if we were both looking for the same constellation we could not be that far away from each other.

Still, I couldn't sleep. During the day we peeled, diced and cooked over twenty pounds of new potatoes that my grandfather dug up just hours earlier, for the potato salad. Sugar Lea made ten of her famous tomato pies. I was responsible for picking the tomatoes for the pies and I sat in the tomato patch in the June heat for a spell and ate two of the tomatoes directly off the vine. Hot tomato juice ran down the sides of my mouth; it was heavenly. Aunt Ivory fried chicken all day long. Papa, that is what we call my grandfather Tom, bought a real nice electric fryer for the occasion at the *Sears & Roebuck*. It was a marvel. He set it up on the back screened-in porch, on top of the canning table, and Aunt Ivory breaded and floured the chicken before dropping it into the hot oil. She was opposed to using the new fryer, but Sugar Lea said there was no other way to do it. The kitchen was large but it was not large enough to hold four women, all with their own way of doing things.

Aunt Topaz was fond of saying Sugar Lea ruled the kitchen like a hen. But that was all right with Aunt Topaz because she preferred sitting on the front porch and reading and listening to her Frank Sinatra records. They put Aunt Topaz in charge of making the vegetable dishes because it did not take much science. I sat with her the day before under the sycamore trees; we must have shelled four bushels of butterbeans and Crowder peas and snapped two bushels of green beans. It was fun because Aunt Topaz told stories about New Orleans and all the other far off cities where she had lived. She told me about old boyfriends, and the night she danced all night at the Coco Cabana in New York City and how Frank Sinatra winked at her.

I could have shelled and snapped for days, lost in her stories. She always made me feel grown-up and important. She already told me she bought me a tube of Bonne Bell lipstick from Woolworth's. I could not wait. I asked her if she would draw a beauty mark above my lip like the one in some of her pictures and she said we would have to ask Momma first. I nodded and realized it would never happen. Momma did not believe in make-up or beauty marks. She was a member of the new Women's Movement at the University, and started going braless, which upset Sugar Lea to no end.

She stayed out later than usual on most nights and had bumper stickers plastered to the back of her 1960 Ford Fairlane that preached her beliefs. This upset Papa. Papa was a Democrat, but he was what was known as a Dixiecrat—mostly a Democrat, but more conservative than the Kennedy's. Momma turned into a liberal democrat seemingly overnight. Things were changing around King's Paradise.

Still I could not sleep. Every time I tried to fall off into the land of dreams I imagined all the gifts I would be getting tomorrow. Sugar Lea said on the invitations it was a birthday party to celebrate the 100th birthday of Fern and the 10th birthday of Camellia. She said, "please no gifts, just your presence is enough," but I secretly yearned for a few gifts. I knew I could count on several from Aunt Topaz, and I prayed that Momma would finally get me the white French Provincial Canopy bed from the Sears catalogue. I had been praying for that bed for at least two years. It was dreamy. All the beds in King's Paradise were old, antique canopy beds. Well, all the beds except Aunt Ivory's and mine.

Aunt Ivory basically slept on an army cot that just fit under the eaves of the attic. She didn't even have a bedside table. She kept books stacked next to the bed and they sort of formed a table. She did not seem to need much in the way of beautiful things, which is fine with me if that is how she wants to live her life. I love pretty things, and I really, really want that canopy bed and a pink princess telephone, but I know the telephone will probably come much later. As it is, if I get any important phone calls, I have to go into the broom closet, which is next to the only phone in the house, because Sugar Lea or someone is always in the kitchen doing something. And to make matters worse, we are on a party line with the Lawrence family, and there are at least forty of them.

They live in a small hollow at the end of our road; there are seven houses total. We are on what you call an eight party line. Some nights, when I am really bored, I pick up the phone very carefully and listen in on their conversations. They never really say anything interesting, but it passes the time away just the same. If Sugar Lea knew I was doing it she would kill me; she is very big on privacy, she has to be.

There are so many of us living at King's Paradise that privacy is one of our top ten rules. "Obey the rights of another person's privacy," Momma likes to yell at Sugar Lea a lot. Lately, Momma and Sugar Lea are doing a lot of yelling; come to think of it, all the women of King's Paradise are doing a lot of yelling. Papa says there are just too many women under one roof. I feel sorry for him most of the time.

Even at nine, I know how to do things most people could never do. I can make wine, put up vegetables while they are fresh off the vine, make pottery, cook and I am also becoming something of a psychic. I get my psychic talents from Sugar Lea, and Sugar Lea got her psychic talents from Mam, and Mam got her talents from her mother. It passes down through the females of the family; Mam says it's because the female is closer to God, and God gives the talent to those inclined to use it.

Uncle Jasper says it is sinful the way we sometimes carry on with fortune telling. However, Mam put him in his place on more than one occasion, so he keeps his opinions to himself now even though he thinks we are all a covey of witches. I think that is why Sugar Lea does not make me go to church any longer. She and Uncle Jasper had their share of fights over the Bible and what it really says. Uncle Jasper drives a big blue Cadillac, and has taken to wearing a toupee on the top of his head, which is now as slick as a worn tire. For a while he did this ridiculous looking comb-over; he wrapped his thin tendrils of hair around his head like Medusa's snakes, round and round until it looked like a beehive hairdo.

Sugar Lea's first cousin, Carol Lea owns her own beauty shop in Hopewell Springs called "Cutting Up With Carol Lea"; she finally talked to Uncle Jasper about how ridiculous his hair looked. He was putting so much pomade on it to keep it in place that flies were naturally attracted to his hair. Well, Cousin Carol Lea told him about a place where he could get a mail order toupee and no one would know about it, so he ordered it and wears it now even in his sleep. Sugar Lea says it is ridiculous how he thinks we don't know he is wearing a wig, even if it is called toupee. Still, he wears it as if he is wearing the crown of a king.

Technically, Uncle Jasper still owns a portion of King's Paradise, but Sugar Lea says even if he is a man of God, it will be a cold day in Hell before he ever moves back in.

12:00 A.M.

June 20, 1963

TOPAZ

"Did you give her too many of those pain pills, Shug," I asked Sugar Lea after being summoned to Mother's room a little past midnight. Mother seemed especially agitated throughout the day. We all knew she wanted to help with her party preparations, but for the past few weeks she had been going downhill. Fast. Ivory and I thought the party wasn't called for, no matter how old Mother was going to be, but Sugar Lea had to have her way as usual, and now she was sitting up with Mother while she complained of chest pains. I wanted to call Dr. Judson to come out and have a look at her, but Shug (that is what I call Sugar Lea, my baby sister) said no. She thought Mother was just tired and high strung from the party and all.

"I only gave her two of the pills, I'll have you know Topaz. Besides, I give them to her when she can't sleep on many nights. I'll also have you know she was talking to me less than one hour ago in a very lucid, direct manner. She was asking all kinds of questions about the party, who all was coming, what we had fixed to eat, she even asked me if I remembered it was Junie's day too," she said as she sank back into the rocker and pushed her hair off her head. It was unusually hot and humid for early June. We were all tired and completely worn out from the last few days. I suspected Shug wished she hadn't invited so many people, but she was doing it all for Mother and Junie of course.

Mother stirred and said something incoherent. Shug and I sat on either side of her in the bed, watching her, counting her breathing. She was in visible pain.

"Shouldn't we call Dr. Judson now?" I asked, my voice full of fear and dread. Even though my Mother was nearing 100, it was still too soon to lose her. She was my rock. Our home was built on her as if commanded by Jesus, just like He put Peter's name on the Vatican.

"Go get her a cool washcloth and bring that pill bottle in here and let me read the directions again; maybe we could give her one more. And check the upstairs linen closet and see if Mary has any bourbon stashed there, I need something to calm my nerves." I climbed off the bed rubbing my hips and realized a shot of bourbon was the answer for tonight's drama.

Shug was in denial; Mother was fading fast, and I will not have her die in pain. Nevertheless, I flew from the room to the bathroom down the hall and found the medicine bottle in the medicine cabinet, and ran the water a few seconds to have it cool and refreshing. (A cool washcloth is, by the way, the cure-all for any malady in the South.) While the water was cooling down I surveyed the linen closet; hiding under the crisp ironed pillowcases was half a bottle of Uncle Jack. I grabbed the bottle, retrieved the washcloth and surveyed my face. I was fading too, like a three day old magnolia in a silver vase. The noise must have awakened Ivory; she descended from her room in the attic wearing her old worn housecoat and a look of worry in her eyes, which was not unusual—Ivory worried about everything. The only time she smiled or laughed was on our weekly night of Gin Rummy, when she won all the money. She was smarter than any of us and loved to gloat. A librarian. She missed out on life and living, and had her nose stuck into the spines of too many books and not enough men's backbones; she choose her pleasures and they happened to be books.

"It's Mother, isn't it?" she asked, grabbing the Jack from my hands and unscrewing the top to take a large needy slug. She handed it back to me and I too took the bottle in my hands and drank until my throat burned and my soul stirred with regret.

"Yes, apparently she has been having chest pains for the past two or three hours and Shug has been feeding her pain pills left over from her hysterectomy two years ago. They must be old and not working, because Mother appears to be in considerable pain," I said as we made it back to the bedroom.

Shug was in the bed with Mother holding her frail, broken body in her arms and crying. How could she have died in those few minutes it took me to retrieve a bottle of medicine and a cold washcloth? Had I taken the slug of Jack and chatted too long with Ivory? It appeared alcohol was once again the cause of pain.

"Go wake Ada Maude, Mary and Tom; let's just let Junie sleep for a while longer. I can't believe it... she is really gone." The tears came with the force of a thunderstorm, only there would be no break in this flood for many days. Mother was gone. I walked over to the bed holding Ivory's hand. We were both shaking and crying. There was great irony in the fact that Mother died in the arms of her favorite child.

JUNIE

I must have fallen asleep, because suddenly I was fully awake and Momma was standing over my bed staring down at me. She had a lost look on her face, like she had fallen off the edge of the world and nobody was there to catch her. She was holding a bottle of Uncle Jack, the secret ingredient for all good things from the kitchen at King's Paradise.

"Momma what's wrong?" She stood taking a long, laborious drink from the bottle and handed it to me.

"Momma, I'm too young for Uncle Jack, Sugar Lee told me she would tan my hide if she ever caught me drinking that stuff?"

"Well, I was ten when I had my first drink, and you're gonna need this tonight, so just hold your nose and take a big gulp. Go on, do it." I took the bottle from her hand, pinched my nose and took a sip of the brown poison, as Ada Maude called it. It burned like vinegar going down, with a taste of molasses and rubbing alcohol.

"Baby, I've got some sad news for you. Mam is dead."

Just like that, she said it as if she was reciting a poem to Mrs. Faucett in second grade. No tears from Momma either; she is not an emotional person. I stood upright beside my bed and pinched myself to make sure I wasn't dreaming. I knew I was awake because my chigger bites started itching from the night before when Momma and I traipsed out to the cow pasture to look for the Southern Cross. It was still not there after two straight nights of looking for it to appear.

"Momma, please say you are just kidding me and hurry and tell me quick before I start crying." My whole entire body was shaking so hard I couldn't will myself to stop. Momma just stood there looking uncomfortable, not knowing what to say. I knew she wanted to hold me close to her and love me but she couldn't. She took another long draw of Uncle Jack and set it down on the floor.

Finally she reached out her arms to me and I threw myself into her small frame; I wanted her to have the soft bosomed chest of Mam. Then we both started wailing. Not small gentle tears but the wails of two mere humans who had lost the dearest person known to them. We sounded like whales mating, and I suppose in a way we were bonding. It took ten years for this mother and daughter to bond, and though it took the loss of a beloved person to do it, I suppose Mam would have approved. I know it grieved her that Momma and I weren't close. We both shook and clung onto each other as if saving each other from breaking in half. After a few minutes of this embrace, Momma pushed me off her like she didn't know me, and set me on the edge of my bed.

"That's enough," she said, turning her attention to the windows across the front of my room, lined with fireflies in mason jars I kept there all summer long. "Get up, put your clothes on and come to Mam's room with me."

She picked up my dirty clothes from the floor and threw them at me, then did something that was strictly prohibited at King's Paradise, she took her pack of Winston cigarettes from her pocket and lit one. She stood, tapping her feet and smoking in my bedroom, all the while looking at the window and chugging down Uncle Jack, yet refusing to go near the window or the telescope. She wanted to look for her constellation, but I suppose at this time it would seem sacrilegious. I could not stop crying, and was having a hard time pulling on my jeans and getting my shirt over my head. Finally, Momma came over to me and with her cigarette clinched between her lips and helped me finish dressing. On the way out of the room,

Momma stubbed out the cigarette on the edge of the door and pushed it back, half smoked, into the pack. She stood in front of me like she wanted to kiss me on my mouth, then said, "Can you smell smoke on my breath?"

"No Momma I can't, but your hair smells like fried chicken and your fingernails look like shit, and your breath smells like you been honkey-tonkin' all night long," I said, knowing she couldn't very well slap me on the face, which was her chosen method of hurting me. My great aunts would see the telltale print of her hand across my already red-swollen face. None of them, including my grandmother knew how to stop my mother's abuse of me. They were all too afraid of her to react, so I got an abundant outpouring of love from them after Momma felt the need to slap me or make me walk the path to the appropriate tree for a switch to use across my bare legs.

She reached out to slap me, then withdrew her hand. We marched in single file to the room next door; it was full of everyone in the world that mattered to me. Aunt Ivory, Aunt Topaz, Sugar

Lea, and Ada Maude were all standing around Mam's bed holding hands and praying *The Lord's Prayer* in unison.

Momma and I stood in the doorway watching, finally joining in the last few verses, *"Lead us not into temptation, but deliver us from evil for Thine is the kingdom, and the power, and the glory forever and ever, Amen."* Aunt Ivory approached us and took the bottle from Mother's hand; she took a long swallow before passing it around to my grandmother, Sugar Lea and Aunt Topaz. They knew better than to pass it to Ada Maude. I was still sobbing, so Ada Maude broke free from their circle, pulled me to her small bosom and rocked me back and forth with all the tenderness that my own Mother lacked.

The silence was warm and still like the night outside the heavily draped windows. Aunt Ivory and Aunt Topaz were still dressed in their nightgowns, but Sugar Lea and Ada Maude wore their Sunday best. Everyone looked tired, sad and defeated; they had all been working so hard for the party which was now only a few hours away. Aunt

Topaz was the first to speak, and her words were directed to Sugar Lea, "You can't make all the decisions for this family, and tonight I say we take a vote and let the five of us decide fair and square; besides, no one will know the difference, as long as we all act like grown-ups and keep our mouths shut. What do you say Ivy?" Ivy was short for Ivory. When Aunt Topaz wanted something from her, she shortened it to Ivy as a special endearment that was intended to sway things her way.

"Well, it isn't technically a lie, if we don't say anything. I worry about the heat, but it could work if we keep ice packs under her dress. We could cover her with a thin blanket." Aunt Ivory was trying hard to contain herself, but she finally gave in to her need to cry, and resumed a great sob that made me start up wailing again.

"What in God's name are all ya'll talking about," Momma said. Everyone shot her a glance, but it was Aunt Topaz who came to her side and took her gently into her arms as if she were cradling the child she never had herself. She had control of the bottle, and placed it into my

Momma's hands like she was giving her the Holy Communion. I imagined she smelled of her beloved Estee Lauder or Jungle Gardenia, and I saw she had carefully applied Helena Rubenstein red to her lips, which gave a nightmarish image to this rather bizarre occurrence.

"Honey," she addressed Momma alone for she knew that ultimately it was my mother who would make the final decision; she was the logical one, "we are going to prepare Mam's body, and put her in the guest room downstairs for the party today. We're not going to announce her death until later tonight, after the party. Everyone who loves her is coming and we'll let them just stand and look from the doorway of the bedroom. The five of us will take turns standing beside her. We'll tell everyone when they arrive she suffered a light stroke and is simply resting, because it won't be a lie—she *has* suffered a stroke or heart attack and she *is*—well technically—resting."

At this point Aunt Topaz started to break-up; she managed with all her might to compose herself, because this was her moment for theatrics—if there had ever been a moment for her to perform. She continued with the authority of Vivien Leigh in *Gone with the Wind*, eating the radish in the garden scene at the end of part one, just before the intermission, "darling, if we do this it won't ruin the day for everyone. Besides, we've all worked like field hands, no offense Ada Maude darling, but well… getting ready for this party, it's what Mam would have wanted. Don't you agree sweetheart? And besides it's your daughter's party too."

Suddenly Momma was the object of ten expectant eyes, as if what she said would be the final verdict. It was *my* party too. I was overcome with emotion and started to bolt from the room and just run, anywhere. Sugar Lea stopped me and held me while I had another good cry; then all of us had another good cry.

"Sweetheart, what do you think?" Aunt Ivory asked. "Have we all totally lost our minds? For once Topaz is right. Besides we have over twenty gallons of potato salad and twenty fried chickens, and my God I forgot about all those tomato pies,

Mother's favorite." She started to cry again. Finally it was Momma who took charge of Sugar Lea and my two distraught great aunts. No one ever took charge of Ada Maude; she was being very quiet and removed from the situation.

"Well I have never heard of a more ridiculous plan in all my entire life!" Momma exclaimed. "Just tell everyone the truth and we can call the party tomorrow a wake."

"Baptists don't have wakes," Aunt Ivory said, taking a long draw of the bourbon before passing it back to Momma, who seemed to be in need of it to make a decision. They all nodded in agreement.

"Then do it," Momma answered, "but I hope you know if you all get into some kind of trouble for this I will have no part of it. I'll lie and say I knew nothing about it. I swear I will not go back to jail. There is bound to be some insane law in the state constitution requiring an accurate time of death, and besides, with the heat tomorrow, well… I hate to be blunt, but I am afraid Mam's body will start to decay."

"We've already thought of that. We decided to use the window unit, put it on full blast, and keep ice on her. No one will get too close anyway 'cause one of us will be with her at all times," Aunt Topaz said as they all seemed to agree in unison this was a done deal.

We all stood around Mam's bed. Sugar Lea pulled the soft blanket from around her small frame and started to undress her. Her ample bosom was revealed to us and her breasts hung like thieves on a cross, neither guilty or innocent, just beautiful and sad. She nursed eight children with those breasts and soothed an entire world with her gentle hugs.

My grandmother, my aunts and my mother began the task of a burial wash. Aunt Topaz brought in a plastic washtub filled with rosewater and added a splash of Jungle Gardenia perfume. Everyone took a washcloth and started washing Mam's body from head to toe.

"In the gates of eternity the black hand and white hold each other with an equal clasp."

—Harriet Elizabeth Beecher Stowe

Aunt Topaz went to Mam's closet and picked out Mam's favorite yellow dress. I could still picture her watching me tumble across the front yard calling me a June Bug.

While the bath proceeded, everyone sobbed quietly while Ada Maude hummed *Amazing Grace* through the entire ritual. Aunt Topaz applied some Max Factor make-up and rouge to Mam's perfect cheekbones to give her a little color. Papa stuck his head in the door a few times and just shook his head back and forth. I was sure he disapproved of the whole idea, but he knew better than to voice his opinion with this room full of women, especially a group of women high on Uncle Jack. They didn't fool me one bit, I knew when anyone had been in the bottle, and on any given night all of them had.

After we finished and Mam was dressed and powdered down with Aunt Topaz's Jungle Gardenia talcum, we lifted her from her bed for the last time and carried her down the hallway, and down the stairs to the guestroom. Aunt Ivory turned the window air conditioning unit on full blast, and Papa brought in a couple of electric fans to keep the air moving. I was sent back up to Mam's room to get her special afghan off the foot of her bed.

The afghan was tangled with the bed sheets and I had to pull the sheet from the foot of the bed to release the afghan. As I did an old looking envelope fell to the floor. I picked it up and it was addressed, "For My Chile." I opened the envelope and found an old hand-written letter that looked like the handwriting of a child or someone who had yet to learn to write in cursive. I started to read the letter, but realized they were waiting for the afghan to complete the final production, so I stuck the envelope into the back of my jeans and decided I would give it to Sugar Lea later when things returned to normal. Would things ever return to normal?

By now it was around 4:00 a.m., and we decided we would try to rest for a couple of hours before getting up to start the final preparations for the party. My aunts and my grandmother looked very tired; Momma already went back to bed. I told them I would sit with Mam in the darkness and watch out for her until they came back downstairs.

Wearily, they started up the stairs when suddenly we heard a loud explosion like a shotgun going off. Everyone flew to the front windows as a great fireball erupted against the night lighting up the room.

Momma ran down the stairs holding Mam's confederate sword in her hand; Papa was right behind her with his double barrel shotgun. Papa was using the Lord's name in vain and Momma was cursing like a sailor. They flung open the front door and there, standing in our yard, was a burning cross with a sign that read, "Nigger Lover Die." Sugar Lea, Aunt Ivory, and Aunt Topaz rushed to Ada Maude and pulled her into a tight circle. I just stood there with my mouth wide-open, catching bugs in my mouth from the light above the front door. I felt the heat from the cross burning and watched helpless as my grandfather and my mother started running down the long driveway to drive away the demons that had done such a horrible thing.

Sugar Lea was in hysterics, screaming for them to come back, fearing for their safety. Momma was swinging the sword like a veteran soldier and Papa fired the shotgun into the seemingly perfect June night. Aunt Ivory and Aunt Topaz yanked and pulled on the hosepipe and tried to put out the flames, but the cross was big, shooting sparks thirty feet into the air. It was a sight I will never forget; the hissing sound of the burning cross was louder than the tree frogs and crickets. I wanted to run somewhere for safety, so I ran into the house and into the guestroom with Mam.

I put her cold hand to my warm face and held it there until it became warm again. It was as if she was alive for just a moment. I was crying and shaking so hard I could not catch my breath.

Ada Maude walked into the room and took me into her arms and we rocked each other back and forth for support as if we had become one person. She took my face into her lined thin hands and told me everything would be all right by morning, and I believed her. I always believed her, why should that night have been any different.

I feel asleep in her arms with her humming *Amazing Grace* into my ear while she fanned my face with the image of Dr. Martin Luther King embossed onto the worn paper fan with the words, *Until Justice Rolls Like a Mighty Stream,* scrawled below his image and an image of Hopewell Spring's Funeral home neatly penned on the bottom.

"God is the free cause of all things."

—Spinoza

THE PARTY

When I awoke, I was in Mam's old bed and someone put a pitcher of freshly picked Gardenias next to me on the bedside table. I could barely smell the smoldering cross on the front lawn. I raced to the window and saw Papa and about ten men still cleaning up the debris the cross had made.

The sheriff and three deputy cars were parked in the front of the house. I still wore my dirty jeans and dirty shirt from the day before. I looked at the clock and it was almost eleven! The party was supposed to start in one hour.

I raced down the stairs to check on Mam; Momma was sitting in the rocking chair beside her reading something. I remembered the letter I found the night before and reached into my pocket to find it was gone. Momma looked up at me as I entered the room and tucked the letter into her lap like something a teacher would do when they found a love letter from two students in second grade. Momma stood up and came to me looking at peace—considering the events of the night before.

"You gonna be O.K. with this today, honey?" She asked.

Momma never called me honey or sweetheart or even Junie. I nodded yes, and took a hard look at my Mother. She seemed very different to me.

"Camellia, I have something I must tell you that isn't going to be easy for me to say, but with the events of last night and the discovery of this letter, well… I don't know if you read the letter, did you?

I shook my head no.

She continued, "I think it is best if we wait until Ada Maude and Sugar Lea come in here because this letter concerns them as well as you."

She left the room, and I had time to sit and watch Mam for a few quiet moments. Mam looked at peace, and looked younger than she had in weeks. I guess she was already in Heaven, and it must agree with her. She probably already found Big Daddy up there, and they were celebrating her birthday together with their two dead children, Uncle Coal and the baby Willow.

Momma, Sugar Lea and Ada Maude walked into the room and shut the door behind them. The hum of the air conditioner and the whirring sound of the fans was all that broke the uncomfortable silence that stood between the four of us.

Sugar Lea spoke first, "Honey, you know we all love you more than anything else in this world, don't you?"

I nodded yes because I really did know that in my heart.

"Well, that letter you found last night in Mam's bed brought to light some news that might be troubling for you, and might be hard for you to understand. But considering what happened here last night, it is something we feel you are ready to hear. Happy Birthday darling, by the way." She cleared her voice and looked between Momma and Ada Maude for reassurance that whatever she was about to say to me was the right thing to say.

I prepared myself, and knew she was going to tell me I was dying with cancer of the brain or of the heart, because my head and my heart were both hurting real bad.

"Ada Maude had a daughter. You know that don't you honey? Her name was Willow, and she was the prettiest girl you ever saw. Grown men would cry when they looked at her, she was so pretty. She was smart, but she was what we call a slow thinker. Ada Maude, I hope you won't mind me saying so will you?"

Ada Maude shook her head no, but she kept her eyes staring straight-ahead, fanning herself with Dr. Martin Luther King, and then she spoke, "I always blamed it on having her at such an old time in my life, 45 was too old to be having a baby, but after watching all the other women with their chuldren, I jess wanted one to my own."

I felt she needed me, so I went over, stood next to her, and put both my arms around her small frame. She squeezed me tight around my middle and I smelled her snuff on her breath and felt comforted. It is funny how scents have always comforted me. Like Gardenia and even the wonderful aroma of a fresh pile of cow manure.

Sugar Lea continued, "Anyway, Willow was beautiful, and like I said, men were drawn to her beauty in odd ways. One night Willow was walking home from town and she was picked up by one of the townsmen and he…" at this point Sugar Lea looked uncomfortable and avoided looking at Ada Maude. I hunkered closer to Ada Maude and felt her arm squeeze me tighter and tighter until I thought I could not breathe at all.

The star Eta Carinae is a star in the Southern sky, near the Southern Cross constellation. In 1843, its brightness increased greatly to magnitude -1, making it the second brightest star in the sky

> *after Sirius. It then became dimmer decreasing to magnitude 6 to 8 until recently when it started climbing in brightness again, reaching 5th magnitude in June 1999. It appears to be going through another phase of rapid brightening and is likely to reach magnitude -1 again in the next few years. This super massive star will one day erupt as a supernova, and when it does, this galaxy will see the biggest bang it has ever seen. This could happen in 10 years or in a hundred million years, no one really knows.*
>
> —Revelation13.net

I felt Ada Maude so close to me that for a moment I forgot Mam and the love I felt for her. I felt Ada Maude and I were one, and if I allowed it, her love could save me from all fear, and from my loss of Mam. I was trusting when it came to love.

Mam told me countless times that love, in the end, was all that mattered. I believed her and I knew in this small room of women I had more love at ten than most people would know in a lifetime.

Sugar Lea took me gently away from Ada Maude's embrace and held me close to her. It was at this time that Momma stood and formed a circle with Ada Maude and Sugar Lea around me.

Momma said it first, "Camellia, Ada Maude is your great-grandmother, just as much as Mam was. She is part of you. You are part of her. Willow was your grandmother, and Willow's son Jackson was your father. We grew up together here at King's Paradise, fell in love and made you. You were our hope and our future. Our little shining star. I am so sorry I have been a horrible Mother, and I hope you can forgive me for not being honest with you all these years."

Momma cried, Sugar Lea cried, yet Ada Maude smiled at me with her bright yellow eyes. My eyes. The eyes of my daddy. MY DADDY!

"How did my Daddy die?" I asked Momma, not knowing if I should run to her arms or stay locked in Ada Maude's stare.

Sugar Lea looked back and forth between the two women and finally said what everyone was so afraid to say, "Junie, your daddy isn't dead; he's on his way to see you right now. Right this very moment he is on an airplane coming to you from Washington D.C. where he has lived for the past few years. When you were conceived, and Honey you were conceived in love, your mother and your daddy loved each other as much as any two people ever loved each other; it was just an impossible love. Things were rough for a while here when word got out that your Momma and Jackson Brown secretly got married by a Justice of the Peace in New York. Your Papa took it really bad too, and especially Uncle Jasper. He preached that we were all going straight to Hell. Then something changed. Your Momma and Jackson moved to New York to live, and they were banished from here. It was hard for them, living so far away from the only home they ever knew, and it was hard on all of us, losing two people we loved so much. Ada Maude already lost Willow; she died giving birth to Jackson in Mam's bed. We brought her into the big bed and took turns watching her for two days. A midwife came, but it was too late. She was just too small to have such a big baby, and she died a horrible death," Sugar spoke without looking at any of us. She avoided Ada Maude at all costs.

I could hear Ada Maude taking shallow breathes that she held in her mouth as if she was holding a fresh wad of snuff. I was having a hard time adjusting to this information. I was only ten!

In the span of twenty-four hours, I lost a great-grandmother who raised me, gained a great-grandmother I didn't know I had, witnessed a cross burning on my front lawn and learned my father was alive. But somewhere in the back of my mind I didn't allow myself to think about the most startling revelation of all—I was a Negro.

If my daddy was a Negro and my great-grandmother was a Negro, then surely I was a Negro too. A Negro.

I heard myself talking for the first time as if I were disconnected from who or what I was. "Was Willow black like you Ada Maude?"

Finally Ada Maude spoke, "I guess we are in a praise the Lord holiness, get-down-to-the-brass-tacks honesty session right now. Hallelujah and Praise Jesus! Willow was half black and half white, just like you Honey Chile. Willow's father was your great uncle Cleveland Cribbs of Covington County. I loved him and he loved me, but he had a family back in Covington and there was no room for a skinny colored woman in his house. So Mam took me and Willow in, then Big Jack married me because he said it didn't matter to him that I had a Mulatto baby. He gave us so much love; he was a good man to marry me and give Willow his name. Cleveland was the prettiest white man you have ever seen, and believe it or not, I was not bad looking in those days either. White mans was always chasing after us colored girls, nobody ever talked about it in open public, but it happened."

At this point Sugar Lea interrupted and told Ada Maude she had said all that was needed to be said.

"So was my Daddy black, or half white too?" I asked.

At this point my Momma stood in front of me with a photograph of a child that looked like my twin brother. He must have been around the age of ten or twelve; it was hard to say because it was an old fashioned looking picture. "This is your Daddy on his tenth birthday," she said, "and as you can see, you look identical to him. We've never known the identity of his father until tonight, when you discovered the letter. Here, go ahead and read it for yourself."

Momma handed me the letter and I went over to the rocking chair next to Mam's body and started to read it when Aunt Topaz knocked on the door to remind us of the time and that guests would be arriving soon.

Everyone left me alone with the letter, everyone except Mam who seemed to love me in spite of her soul already being in Heaven. I opened the one page letter and read:

Dear chile, when you reed this liter I will mos likly be deed an gon, for I no the lord is cuming for me. I hop He savs you and I hop you will somday now I wil always be watching you from heaven. Your dady is not whu they think he is, your dady is Jasper. He loves me and Jesus loves me and I am going hom.

I love you,

Your Muther, Willow Maude

It took a long time to read the letter, for the paper was yellowed and the spelling crude and simple, like a first grader. It was hard for me to understand how a mother could write with so many misspelled words. Uncle Jasper? Now I am really confused, and I'm only ten! My Uncle Jasper is really my grandfather too. Jasper and Willow were married? Why hadn't anyone told me this before? So, Momma and Daddy were cousins? Isn't that bad? And Daddy is coming tonight to meet me. Why now?

I ran from the guestroom to search for Momma and get all the facts straight. I heard unfamiliar voices coming from the hallway and decided it was best to sneak up the back staircase and have a hot bath and get on my party dress that Momma bought for me at the J.C.Penney's store in town last week. I hated wearing dresses, but considering it was such a special day, I conceded to wear it. I felt foolish; just imaging how silly I'll look in it.

I had the entire second floor to myself, so I started peeling off my clothes before I made it to the bathroom. I went into the bathroom, looked at myself in the mirror hanging from the medicine cabinet, and saw myself for the first time as a Negro girl.

So what and who was I really? Half Negro, Half White, Cherokee princess. Was I more white than Negro or more Negro than white? I realize now why I had few friends in school and why I was never invited to sleepovers and parties like the other girls my age. I wasn't angry. I was confused.

Someone knocked on the door, and Momma stood in the doorway looking fresh and almost pretty in the one good dress she owned. Her hair was pulled up on top of her head and it appeared she was wearing lipstick.

"Want me to wash your back?" She asked timidly.

"I guess so," was all I could think to say.

It felt luxurious and comforting for us to be alone in the steamy bathroom. I wanted us to stay like this forever. We did not say another word the entire time. After she washed my back, she picked up a pitcher of water, added a few drops of Aunt Topaz's rosewater, and poured it through my thick head of hair, which was falling like the weight of the world around my shoulders.

There were a million questions in my head and I felt I deserved answers, but I was too tired to ask, and I felt Momma was too afraid to answer. She cleaned my hair with sweet smelling shampoo and started humming a song. Momma never hummed. There was a knock at the door, and there stood Aunt Topaz looking just like Elizabeth Taylor. Her scent preceded her by a good four feet. She smiled at the scene she was witnessing and had a wrapped package in her hand.

"Excuse me for interrupting, but I wanted Junie to have this gift so she could use it before the party. Honey, I love you. And I just want you to know all this will pass. You are my sweetheart, and I love you so much I would kill for you if need be, but… well, anyway, open your little present and come down, you have guests arriving and they are bearing gifts for the princess on her birthday." She winked, causing her heavily massacred eyelashes to flutter and almost stick together, then slipped out of the room; though the scent of Jungle Gardenia stayed, almost smothering me.

Without speaking, Momma picked up a thick sun-dried towel and wrapped my skinny body into the sweet smelling folds. The towel felt rough and comforting to me as Momma rubbed off the last hint of rosewater from my skin. I flipped my head down for her to wrap the towel turban style around my hair.

We padded down the hall to my bedroom and in place of my old twin bed stood the white-canopied bed I dreamed of owning for the past two years. It was complete with a white eyelet bedspread and an assortment of colored pillows. I turned to Momma and she shrugged her shoulders as if to say, 'I really do love you.' I ran to my new bed and jumped into the middle, being careful not to hurt the white eyelet canopy that stood over my head like a beautiful white sky.

"A bed doesn't make up for what you have been through over the past twenty-four hours, but at least you will have a special place to rest tonight after all this party stuff is over," Momma said as she sat next to me.

"And after everyone leaves, before your Daddy gets here, we can sneak off to look for our Southern Cross if you want to."

I was suddenly overcome with so many different feelings and emotions I couldn't contain myself, and I started to cry. She cradled me in her arms and rocked me as best she could. I let her hold me and I let her try to love me.

The party was a success, although I remained most of the day in the guestroom watching over Mam. Various kinfolk wandered in to look at her while standing in the doorway, remarking how peaceful she looked in her sleep. Uncle Jasper did not come to the party, which was a relief to me. I learned later that Sugar and Papa paid him a visit in the early morning hours and threatened him not to show his face again at King's Paradise. I could never look at him the same way again anyway. I could never really look at anyone the same way again. I would look at everything differently, and I realized it would be much better now that I knew I had a daddy and a new great-grandmother who already loved me. Mam told me many times that the Lord never gave you more than you could handle and trials and tribulations only made you stronger.

I felt nervous about meeting my daddy, who was supposed to arrive around nine o'clock tonight. He would fly into Birmingham, rent a car, and drive the hour and one-half to Hopewell Springs.

Momma told me the truth about what happened to them as we were sitting together watching over Mam. "We were so young and so naïve, thinking color wouldn't matter if we lived in New York; it was the melting pot of America and the two of us with you were indeed a melting pot. We thought we would be safe there, find a way to make a family and make our love work. I was cut off from Sugar, Papa, everyone here, and of course we broke Ada Maude's heart by leaving; I knew things would be so difficult if we stayed. Honey, black men were lynched for looking at a white woman's legs in those days. I loved your daddy too much to risk losing him, and I didn't want to bring shame on Sugar and Papa. Your daddy didn't leave me, I left him. You and I came back here when you were almost two; I felt like I had lost my best friend and gained the world at the same time. I was home, and I knew I did the right thing by coming home. Your daddy wrote to me every day, begging me to come back to him. There are few things I got right in my life, but you, and moving back here to have you raised by Sugar Lea, Ada Maude and Mam was the best thing I have ever done. After a year of living alone, your daddy started school at the University of Virginia; I took the train to see him three or four times, but we still had to meet in secret, and it was a burden on Sugar knowing where I was… and I hated leaving you behind.

"Whatever you think or believe about my feelings for you… I just love you so much, but things were so messed up inside my head most of the time, I didn't know how to show you." Momma looked down the entire time she was talking to me; I felt relieved she wasn't looking into my face because fat, hot tears were streaming down my face no matter how hard I tried to restrain myself. She was brave to tell me the truth; I felt I should be brave and not cry. I could not help it though. Somewhere deep inside me a well had sprung and it was filling up my eyes quicker than I had time to wipe the tears away. She looked at me, took her sweet hands, and wiped away as many of my tears as she could. We both looked over at Mam's face for consolation as we had done so many times before, but there was nothing to be gained from our stares.

Aunt Topaz stuck her head in the room and informed us it was time to eat; we begrudgingly stopped our conversation, and I asked Aunt Topaz to please bring me a plate of tomato pie and a glass of sweet iced tea. I was not hungry, but I felt dizzy, and Momma and Aunt Topaz decided it was best if I ate something.

I sat deep inside the rocking chair and felt the gentle motion of the creaky rockers hitting the pine floor. I loved the sound. It was a memory sound I stole from my earliest recollections and placed it in a special place near my heart. Mam and Ada Maude rocked me to sleep almost every night when I was still small enough to fit under their arms. As I grew, we were a sight to behold. My long legs sticking out like a cricket legs, brown and golden from the sun. But we rocked nonetheless. Rocking and rocking. We did not talk, we were deep in our thoughts of the universe, solving the problems of the world. Two wise old women and one gangly half-Negro, half-white, part Cherokee girl. They knew all along, and neither one of them ever gave me a clue as to the secret of myself. Before too many minutes, I fell asleep

When I awoke, I was in my new canopy bed and Momma was lying beside me. I could tell from the light outside it was twilight. I could hear the Alabama summer sounds outside my windows and my fireflies were beating themselves against the bell jars.

I crept out of my bed trying not to wake Momma and opened the jars one by one, releasing the fireflies into the warm Alabama air. The night was clear and I could tell it was going to be a perfect night for stargazing.

Most of the guests had left, there were a few cars left in the yard scattered around various places and I could hear the clang of some men still playing horseshoes on the side of the house. It was a perfect night. For a few moments, I forgot about Mam's death and my new identity. I could see the lights of a car heading down the long driveway and realized it was the local funeral parlor's long black hearse.

I ran down the stairs and found Sugar Lea, Aunt Ivory, Aunt Topaz and Ada Maude standing in the front hallway waiting. When they saw me, they all held open their arms for me to choose whom I wanted to hold me. I choose Sugar Lea. I knew Ada Maude would understand, I figured Sugar Lea needed hugs more than anyone else did, after what she had been through over the past ten years. Especially over the past twenty-four hours. We both cried, and then all five of us cried as the knock came at the door.

Aunt Topaz opened the door to Clyde Stevens, the undertaker. He lifted his hat and asked where Mam was.

The five of us escorted him to the guest room where she was laid out. None of us went into the room with him. He came out after a few minutes and his two helpers brought in a long black stretcher to take her body away. We went into the kitchen and started the chore of cleaning up from the party. No one said a word. Sniffles and sobs broke through the sound of glasses clanging and plates being washed.

I heard the front door close and heard the hearse drive away with Mam, and we all walked in silence out onto the front porch to watch her leave King's Paradise for the last time. We all shook and cried and held onto each other like the world was about to end. And it had.

Momma walked out onto the porch to join us. The sky had turned into a charcoal twilight. She carried her portable telescope in her arms and had on her old jeans full of holes and patches that were like second skin to her. We had all shed our party clothes and felt so relieved to do so. Momma motioned for me to join her.

We walked down the driveway past the front pasture and climbed through our opening in the barbed wire fence. We had worn a deep path in the summer clover. The night smelled of clover, honeysuckle, tobacco grass and dew. I had so many different emotions dancing in my brain; I felt at any moment I would break down and cry. So much had happened and so much was still about to happen; I had lost Mam, but I was gaining a father. I didn't want to believe God had made it all happen, but something had certainly changed my life in the past twenty-four hours. I saw God as a puppet master sitting on the edge of Heaven, directing earth with strings and circumstance. It would be years before I made decisions based on fact and reasoning. For now, I was fine with God being a puppeteer. It was comforting somehow to believe in a God that actually controlled the world in such a personal way. I began to question the existence of one god and realized there could be a million gods, perhaps they were even the stars. Momma certainly worshiped the stars, but then again she also loved Jesus.

"Momma why do you love the stars so much? I have always been afraid to ask that question, but since we are all so open and honest now, I would like to know," I asked as we walked in the thigh-high grass, dodging fresh cow piles.

"Well honey, I started loving the stars after I left your daddy. They became my friends and I started a love affair with them," She giggled, imagine Momma giggling, "I would come out here most nights after I put you to bed and cry. With their brilliance they spoke to me of finding a better tomorrow. I figured if a star led them to Jesus, Jesus could lead me by the stars. I didn't know where I was going, but I knew I was on a journey going somewhere. One day by accident I was reading the World Book Encyclopedia out of boredom, trying to figure out what I wanted to study and become, and found the section on the constellations. I was intrigued, and just like that, I decided I would study astronomy; and then of course by fate, I stumbled onto the Southern Cross and all the folklore around it. Everything fell into place, I suppose as Mam would say by 'Divine Provenance'."

"Okay" was all I could muster to say, for we had already started setting up the telescope and watching the horizon for the Southern Cross.

"Momma what does Daddy do up there in Washington, D.C., and do you still love him? Do you think he will love me?"

"Honey, your daddy is an attorney with the President's brother, Attorney General Robert Kennedy. Your daddy is a very important person right now. And very smart. Want to know why he's finally coming home? When Mr. Kennedy found out he grew up so close to Tuskaloosa, he decided to send him down here to help out with some of the problems at the University. But someone in town found out about him coming home, and that's why we had a cross burned in our yard last night. But don't worry, when your daddy gets here we'll all be safe. He's bringing federal marshals with him just to guard our house for the next few weeks.

"Yes I will always love your daddy, and yes he loves you. We speak to each other as often as possible and he kept up with you through Ada Maude. Remember every summer when she tells you she is visiting a cousin in Atlanta? Well she travels by train to visit Jackson in Washington and they have a wonderful time. I haven't seen him in almost five years, so I'm a little nervous. I suppose I could use a little of Aunt Topaz's cosmetic skills right now, but that is what is so wonderful about your daddy and Me, we love each other with our souls. He would love me if I was purple with pink polka dots and I would love him if he were green with red polka dots." We both giggled and I felt happier than I had in my entire life.

"Why is Daddy bringing federal marshals with him Momma? Are we expecting another cross burning," I asked.

Momma shifted her position and pushed the telescope to me. I could tell by her smile she had found it. The one thing that held us together, the other cross that would never let us down. The new Star of Bethlehem. Guiding us, promising us great things if we would only believe and receive the promises inside ourselves.

I looked into the telescope and found the constellation just rising over the horizon as if to make amends for what had transpired over the past twenty-four hours.

Momma put her arms around me and we stood there in the stillness. Smiling. Watching. Waiting. Wishing and hoping. Always hoping. Always dreaming of the promise of a better tomorrow, here at the foot of the Southern Cross at King's Paradise.

Down the long, winding driveway the lights of a car approached. I stood up, grabbed Momma's hand and we ran, skipping, jumping over clover to meet my daddy. My heritage. A new beginning. We forgot the telescope and for several days after there was no mention at all of our constellation.

We were in our own Heaven.

"I am a dreamer. I am, indeed, a practical dreamer. My dreams are not airy nothings. I want to convert my dreams into realities, as far as possible."

—Monhand as Karamchand, (Mahatma Gandhi)

Our heaven lasted one week. I came to love my daddy and pretended he would stay at King's Paradise forever. He couldn't. More importantly, we could not be a real family. We could not be the family I so often dreamed of having. I was to live in Purgatory forever. I decided I was destined to live out the remainder of my life as someone floating above the earth like my Mother's constellation. I began to hate everything and everyone. Life was not fair. I lost Mam and now my father in the space of one week. Ada Maude tried to help me understand. She would pull me into her thin frame and hold me until I had cried all the tears I thought possible in the world. I was drowning in my misery and in my pain.

Ada Maude encouraged me to walk the land and feel nature. Momma let me miss school the entire week Daddy left to return to Washington. King's Paradise felt like a garrisoned castle in the middle of a medieval war. The cross burnings in our yard continued for months. Even with Grandpa Tom standing watch from the front porch with his shotgun in his arms, and Momma standing watch from her bedroom window with Mam's sword by her side, next to the box of Kleenex. She had her cigarettes with her at all times during these days, and Sugar Lea consented to her smoking in her room only. Her room had a thick veil of smoke that clung to her clothes, her hair and her fingers. I hated seeing her like this, but she kept us all at arm's length. She was heartbroken that my father left her. And Mam's death created a black shroud around our house like a tightly woven cocoon. We were all grieving for her in our own way.

Sugar Lea stayed busy putting up vegetables from the garden, Aunt Topaz sat on the porch listening to her Frank Sinatra records and Aunt Ivory stayed in her room all day reading mystery novels and drinking cherry coca-colas.

Me, I just sat at Ada Maude's feet and read to her about the changing world while dodging her tobacco spits and feeling blessed I still had her.

I promised my daddy I would write him a letter every day of the week; I missed two days because I had to have my tonsils out and my mother said Daddy would understand. Daddy promised he would write to me often, and even try to call me sometimes. We didn't have any real time alone together, but before he left he walked with me to Ada Maude's old cabin behind our house. The kudzu had already started the ascent up the walls of the house and it looked like it was probably filled with snakes and spiders, but Daddy said he wanted to see it again. He told me it helped him to be there. He said if he had stayed at King's Paradise he would never be the person he was supposed to be. He said he felt God had chosen him to set his race free, just as Dr. King was trying to do. He told me things were going to be hard for me now that I was part Negro, but I didn't feel any different. I knew who I was, and being half Negro did not and could not change me. I was already me long before I learned the truth about my origins.

Several months after the incident at King's Paradise, my Mother decided it was best for the two of us to move out of King's Paradise to the city of Tuskaloosa and closer to the University. She also felt it was time for her to find a man to love. Sugar Lea had a full-time job nursing Ada Maude after the death of Mam. Ada Maude passed peacefully two months Mam's death in her sleep, just as Mam had. We buried her in the family plot next to Mam where she deserved to be.

We were all relieved that Ada Maude passed before the Kennedy brothers and Dr. King were assassinated. Momma said Ada Maude secretly predicted Dr. King would be shot and that is why she went on to be with God. Her heart had been broken so many times.

Daddy came to the funeral and brought along a woman named Ava with him. I believe it killed my Mother's spirit, for she loved him with her whole entire soul. He was moving up in the political world and needed to start a family to make himself electable to the masses.

He couldn't very well walk around with his white wife and his "mixed" daughter, could he? He was kind to me and continued to write me long letters outlining his views on Civil Rights and Justice. Before Dr. King's assassination, Dr. King had chosen my daddy, Jackson, to be on his legal team, and my daddy was often in the newspapers, but I was to pretend he was just someone I knew from my past at King's Paradise.

Momma adjusted to Daddy's fame and fortune and began to change. She had her hair cut short and started wearing dresses and even bought herself a tube of Aunt Topaz's Helena Rubenstein red lipstick. Aunt Topaz was delighted to help Momma improve her personal image and gave her instructions on how to apply base foundation, eye liner and even mascara. It took some getting used to, but Momma was coming out of her shell and trying to love me like mothers are supposed to. On Saturdays we would go into town to see movies. We would sink deep into the theatre seats and sip on our coke and watch the same movie sometimes three or four times.

For the briefest period, Momma forgot about the stars in the heavens and loved me. She missed the stars, and I missed the mother she was when she had them. I gave them back to her.

I love life. I have decided it is what you make it. I am indeed a practical dreamer. And someday Momma says my daddy could even become President of the United States.

Imagine.

And I am still the keeper of "the secret" told to me those days preceding the death of Mam and all the confusion which followed. I am holding onto the secret because I figure one day it will make one hell of a book. I have decided I want to be a writer when I grow up, a keeper of history, a voice of justice, a visionary. A visionary.

January 21, 2003

SISTER CAMILLE

I sit in row 3 of Flight 80, Atlanta to Washington D.C. I am the only person on the plane. It seems unreal and a bit frightening to me, for I have never really taken to the skies as my mother did. I am 50 years old. I chose to give my life to God after my Mother died an early death; I became a nun at St. Francis Convent in New Orleans, Louisiana. I feel I am needed there for there are many children who roam the streets homeless, motherless and fatherless. I know what that feels like to a degree, but I put all those thoughts out of my head and my heart, and have moved forward in my life. I took the name Sister

Camille in deference to my many relatives named Camellia. They are gone now, all of them. It was like a stack of dominoes, once the first one fell the others started tumbling and tumbling and tumbling until only I was left. They are all with me in my heart and in my head, which holds a wealth of memories I cherish and know made me the person I am today. So who did I become? Did I become a white teenager taking the easy route, or did I stand with my black brothers and sisters and keep the revolution rolling? I took no stand on my race. I let people believe what they wanted to believe because my Sugar Lea told me before she died that no matter what race I claimed, people would believe what they wanted to believe and there was no changing ignorance. She said once ignorance got the hold on a person that person was marked forever to be cast into their own private hell on earth. So I just remained Junie, until the day I became Sister Camille, taking my vows at the convent on my 30th birthday. My father was there, and he cried with me when I realized how alone I felt for the first time in my life. Then I remembered how I could do or be anyone, and how special I felt that God had reached out and touched me with a few very strong nudges, and led me to live a life of celibacy and service. When I realized how significant this was, I recognized it was like coming home, really coming home, just like King's Paradise; the convent was a rambling house with many rooms and many women all still very strongly opinionated, and it felt right. It is right.

I continued my love of astronomy, and ended each day with a walk along the sidewalks surrounding the convent, just so I could get a closer look at the stars, knowing that most likely, Heaven is beyond the stars, beyond the Milky Way and far beyond my mother's Southern Cross.

Now I am on my way for my earthly father to introduce me to the world. I told my Mother Superior. I had to tell her; I couldn't have her falling down with a heart attack when she heard the news from the television she kept in her room, her only vice—watching *Jeopardy* each night after Vespers.

I don't know what to expect when I am presented to the world, so to speak. But my father told me it would be the first task on his agenda if he was elected President. I doubt my life will really change; I'll stay a few days, then go back to St. Francis and resume my duties as a good nun. I carry with me a photograph of Mam, Ada Maude, Sugar Lea, Aunt Topaz, Aunt Ivory, my Mother and me, about a month before Mam died that night in her sleep and we pulled off the dramatic birthday party. I keep it with me at all times. In the photograph we are all smiling and Aunt Topaz has her tongue stuck out with her skirt hiked up in the front, always playing the role of a jester, or whichever part needed to be played at that moment. I look very young, and I also look very black. It is hard for me to believe I never really saw myself before I learned the truth of my race on the night the first cross was burned on our lawn—when the truth of my heritage was revealed. No one ever asked me if I was black or white, no one in fifty years, and if by chance someone had asked me, I had the answer on the tip of my tongue ready for a reply. "I am black and I am white and I am a child of God." No one ever asked, and after tomorrow, quite a few people will be very surprised.

The lights of Washington are beneath me now; I suppose I should be nervous and excited and a little scared, but I'm too busy looking at the stars, waiting for the sign of the Southern Cross and all it promises for not only me, but for this wonderful world.

THE END

EPILOGUE

Who is to say what is true, or what is truth, or what truth looks like. Many people believe truth is white or black, and some say truth is only Christian, while others believe truth to be Muslim, Hindu, or some other religion. There is no universal truth, and no universal God; no religion has a monopoly on God. But there is a universal code of decency and we all have a moral obligation to tell our own story, our perception, of what may or may not be truth no matter how painful it may seem, because your perception *is* your truth. And your reality.

The alleged sisterhood of Coretta Scott King and Lady Bird Johnson is an Alabama urban legend. Is it the truth? That can only be determined with DNA testing. This novel is a work of fiction. There are many people who have lived within these pages, and there are many incidents in this book which are acts of truth.

I was first given the "secret" regarding the unlikely sisterhood of Coretta Scott King and Lady Bird Johnson by a man who lived in Selma during the Civil Rights Movement. He posed a simple question, "why Selma?" With the widespread Civil Rights unrest and demonstrations, and all the places Lyndon Johnson could have invoked marshal law, why did he choose Selma, Alabama? There are people who claim that during the time the Federal Marshalls were in Selma, they systematically purged the public records, carried out boxes and boxes of files and did away with them in government vans. But *why Selma*?

Within a 30 mile radius of the fictional town of Hopewell Springs lay the towns of Selma, Billingsly (where the Patillo farm—Lady Bird's maternal family farm—was located), Marion and Heiberger. (Both Marion and Heiberger claim to be the birthplace of Coretta Scott King; unfortunately, there is no record of Coretta Scott Kings' birth.) Billingsly was no more than a bump in the highway, in the county of Autauga; the county seat at that time was Autaugaville, a small town with a small courthouse. Marion and Heiberger are in the county of Perry. Marion is again a relatively small town; it is the county seat and home to Judson College and Marion Military Institute, and was the site of Jimmie Lee Jackson's brutal death which instigated the March from Selma to Montgomery. Coretta Scott King grew up in Marion; she and Martin Luther King married in Marion. Would not Marion be a more fitting starting place for the March than Selma?

Selma, the county seat of Dallas County, is about 25 miles from Marion as the crow flies. Many of the records of the neighboring counties of Autauga and Perry were kept in Selma because Selma was a much larger city with better record keeping facilities. Early record keeping in Alabama was informal; recording births, deaths and marriages was not officially required until 1908. Most births around the time of Coretta Scott King's infancy were at-home births, often with the assistance of a mid-wife or sometimes a country doctor. Alabama birth records are legally confidential and cannot be accessed by non-family members for a period of 125 years after the date of birth. Although confidential, the birth records for Coretta Scott King could have been stored at the Dallas County Records department in Selma, and may have linked her to her alleged half-sister, Lady Bird Johnson, through a common father, Thomas Jefferson Taylor.

Lyndon Johnson was an unlikely supporter of civil rights. Throughout his career, the Texas Democrat showed no inclination to support civil rights. There was no reason for him to do so; his constituency generally opposed civil rights. I believe he was led to the Movement through encouragement from Lady Bird and his desire for a historical legacy. In a critical phone call on King's birthday in 1965, King suggested to

Johnson that a coalition of blacks and moderate whites united over the racial integration agenda could win the South, after losing it in the 1964 election when the Deep South states went for Barry Goldwater, the Republican candidate. Following this conversation, King began building pressure in Selma, Alabama, to create very specific situations as a catalyst for change. *Why Selma*?

I propose King and Johnson wanted to suppress the connection between their wives, believing it would tarnish the Movement's legitimacy and threaten its potential success. They conspired to make Selma the civil rights focal point in order to allow Johnson to instigate marshal law, seize the court house records and forever hide Coretta and Lady Bird's sisterhood from public scrutiny.

I, like any good journalist or writer, will not reveal my sources, and I do not claim this book is only a figment of my imagination. I wrote Junie's story years ago and kept it in the back of my mind. When I became privy to the information regarding

President Johnsons' raid on the Dallas County Courthouse in Selma, I knew it fit with the geography, era and civil rights theme of this book

There is nothing more scared than a sister, and I know if there was the slightest, most remote chance there was a sister out there I never knew—or perhaps knew, yet not as a sister, but as an equal woman of power—I would want to know about it. Look at the Hemings family and Thomas Jefferson; they are a now a complete circle.

I like to think Coretta Scott King and Lady Bird Johnson knew about their sisterhood. I like to think it was one of the driving forces behind Lady Bird's encouragement of Lyndon Johnson to fight for the right of Blacks to vote. I like to think someday there will be an end to this urban legend and someone will be courageous enough to seek DNA testing.

Coretta Scott King and Lady Bird Johnson

CIVIL RIGHTS TIMELINE

This story, though a work of fiction, was shaped by a series of events casting the shadow that would become Southern life in the 1960s. I know, because I lived this story. My life was shaped by the crescendo of fear fueled by ignorance, prejudice and the assassinations of four leaders who offered hope and direction to a world steeped in traditions of oppression and injustice. I wrote this story so my grandchildren and future generations will know truth and justice, and for those who suffered. I offer my sorrow, my apologies and my hope for a brighter future on this, the 50th anniversary of George Wallace's historic stand in the schoolhouse door on the campus of The University of Alabama. George Wallace offered his own apologies before he passed away in 1998. We are all redeemed if we ask.

June 19, 1865—*Juneteenth*, is considered the date when the last slaves in America were freed. Although the rumors of freedom were widespread prior to this, actual emancipation did not come until General Gordon Granger rode into Galveston, Texas and issued General Order No. 3, on June 19th, almost two and a half years after President Abraham Lincoln signed the Emancipation Proclamation.

August 28, 1955—Emmett Till, a 14 year old African American boy from Chicago, inadvertently started the Civil Rights movement. Hard to imagine, yet true. Emmett traveled to Money, Mississippi in August of 1955 to visit relatives when he was brutally murdered after he "flirted" with a married Caucasian woman.

December 1, 1955—In Montgomery, Alabama, Rosa Parks refused to obey bus driver James F. Blake's order that she give up her seat in the colored section to a white passenger, after the white section was filled. Parks was not the first person to resist bus segregation. Others had taken similar steps, including Irene Morgan in 1946, Sarah Louise Keys in 1955, and Claudette Colvin nine months before Parks. NAACP organizers believed that Parks was the best candidate for seeing through a court challenge after her arrest for civil disobedience.

October 15, 1962—Beginning of the Cuban Missile Crisis; school children in the southeastern United States spend hours acting out bomb drills preparing for the worst.

June 11, 1963—Alabama's Governor George Wallace came to national prominence when he kept a campaign pledge to stand in the schoolhouse door to block integration of Alabama public schools. Governor Wallace read this proclamation when he first stood in the doorway to block the attempt of two black students, Vivian Malone and James Hood, to register at the University of Alabama. President John F. Kennedy federalized the Alabama National Guard, and ordered its units to the university campus.

September 15, 1963—The explosion at the African-American church in Birmingham, Alabama which killed four young girls, marked a turning point in the U.S. 1960s Civil Rights Movement and contributed to support for passage of the Civil Rights Act of 1964.

November 22, 1963—President John F. Kennedy is assassinated by Lee Harvey Oswald (and perhaps others according to conspiracy theories).

February 21, 1965—Assassination of Malcolm X.

March 7, 1965—*Bloody Sunday*, when 600 civil rights marchers, protesting against the death of Jimmie Lee Jackson and the ongoing exclusion from the electoral process, were attacked by state and local police with billy clubs and tear gas. Jimmie Lee Jackson was a deacon of the St. James

Baptist Church in Marion, Alabama, ordained in the summer of 1964. His desire to vote led to his death at the hands of an Alabama State Trooper, and inspired the Selma to Montgomery marches.

The second march, the following Tuesday, resulted in 2,500 protesters turning around after crossing the Edmund Pettus Bridge.

The third march started March 16. The marchers averaged 10 miles a day along U.S. Route 80, known in Alabama as the "Jefferson Davis Highway". Nearly 8000 protesters started the march, protected by 2,000 soldiers of the U.S. Army, 1,900 members of the Alabama National Guard under Federal command, and many FBI agents and Federal Marshals in Selma. The marchers swelled to over 25,000 by the time they reached the Alabama State Capitol Building on March 25.

Martial law was declared in Selma by President Lyndon Baines Johnson. US Marshals seized command of the Dallas County Courthouse, the county seat of Selma.

April 4, 1968—Dr. Martin Luther King is assassinated by James Earl Ray (and perhaps others); Ray later recanted.

June 5, 1968—U.S. Senator and Presidential candidate Robert F. Kennedy is shot by Sirhan Sirhan; he died 26 hours later.

March 10, 1995—Former Alabama Governor George Wallace apologizes for his segregationist ideals at the thirtieth anniversary of the Selma-to-Montgomery march.

I would like to add a side note; I attended Judson College in Marion in the early 1970's and found the culture regarding African Americans had changed little from the 1960's.

Alabama Jane Brown
January 20th 2013 (2nd Inauguration day of
President Barrack Obama)
Tuscaloosa, Alabama

I dedicate this novel to my brave sister, Joanna McGee Byrd who lived with a heart/double lung transplant for 21 years and left this earth on May 3, 2013. I can only hope that by now she has passed *The Southern Cross* and made her way to her own heaven where she is whole. And where one day, I will join her again.

INSIDE THE RABBIT HOLE

For Joanna

You are alive today, still young & brave.
Today do not fear tomorrow and the perceived sorrow;
Do not borrow or steal the doom they have put into your ears
You are alive today, still young & brave.

Do not allow them to take away one molecule from the air you breathe.
Today the air is free & the eternal beauty of the sky is yours alone
If you want to possess it--take it, it is yours.

For today:
We will throw out the rules of life we learned at sixteen,
We will eat more mayonnaise & fried chicken.
We will walk in the rain with our heads uncovered.
We will read through the night with our flashlights burning beneath the sheets.

We will cross the street in the middle of the block
and not bother to walk to the corners.

Let's make a pact, the two of us
When we leave lets
Take a piece of the sky & we will know where to
find each other.
Like Alice, we will tumble & tumble & tumble
for a while
Caught in a place foreign & mysterious.

In this place the air will be illimitable & free, and
will smell of
Honeysuckle, magnolia & gardenia;
This scent will now fill your now perfect lungs.
Just remember to
Hold onto that piece of sky
For it will never, ever die.

If only someone had told us this before today,
The more we live the less we die & the more we die
the less we live.
We would have bought acres & acres & acres of
the sky.

Alabama Jane Brown was born and raised in Tuscaloosa and Northport, Alabama. She received her BA from Judson College for Women, and studied fiction writing with Barry Hannah at The University of Alabama while pursuing an MFA in Creative Writing. Ms. Brown divides her time between an historic farm in Tennessee and a historic log cabin in Alabama with a menagerie of ghosts, cats and grandchildren. Ms. Brown has published on web del sol under "New Voices" and is at work on her third novel, *Montauk*.

www.alabamajanebrown.com